Where Is My Black Belt?

Written by
Grandmaster Seung Dong

PublishAmerica
Baltimore

First printing

ISBN: 1-4137-8132-2
PUBLISHED BY PUBLISHAMERICA, LLLP
www.publishamerica.com
Baltimore

Printed in the United States of America

I would like to dedicate this book to my two uncles. First, I would like to dedicate it to Dr. Edward Jung, and his wife, Jae Ryun Jung, who live in the United States and are celebrating their fiftieth wedding anniversary. Dr. Jung has been my mentor, role model, and inspiration for most of my life. God bless him and his wife, and may they continue to have a long and happy life together. I also would like to dedicate this book to my "young uncle," Dr. Young Ju Jung, who lives in Korea and who was the first person to teach me how to kick and punch when I was very small. He introduced me to martial arts and started me on what was to become my life's work and passion.

Preface

Years ago, when I was driving to my martial arts school, I saw a squirrel sitting beside another squirrel lying dead in the road. As I passed, the squirrel did not run away. It just sat there looking at the still body of the dead squirrel. It did not care about the cars passing by. The squirrel kept staring at the dead squirrel as if it was waiting for its friend to wake up.

I thought that this behavior was very unusual so I pulled over to the side of the road to watch how long the squirrel would sit there. The squirrel continued to watch the body as cars swerved around into the other lane.

It seemed as if the squirrel were shouting, *"Wake up! Let's go!"* That's what I heard from that scene. I was surprised and watched for almost half an hour. The squirrel ran to the curb only a few times to avoid the danger of passing cars. I expected the squirrel to leave that dead friend. I was wrong. I had to be on my way, but that scene has never been erased from my mind.

I have not forgotten that squirrel, because it made me appreciate the innocence, love, and companionship in the animal world. As a human, I look at myself and ask, "Am I better than that squirrel? Would I sacrifice my life for another? Could I love someone that much?"

In 1971, I came to America as a young man with a dream. Since then I have been teaching martial arts. I have met many different people with many different lifestyles. However, I have found that there are two types of people: those that are selfless and those that are self-centered. Fortunately, I have had the privilege to work with many selfless people.

In this story, I would like to share my imagination with you. As far as I can see, no matter where we live or what we are doing, we are all pilgrims in this life together.

I appreciate the support of my family, Mike Edwards, Joan Neff, Lisa Edmonds and the many students that helped make this book possible.

I dedicate this story to all who love the martial arts and future martial artists.

Foreword

As a martial artist, I have devoted my life's work in America to the instruction of my students for over three decades. Through this book, I want to share with my readers the "never give up" attitude or my philosophy of the "**three V's**":

- **One Vision**: the desire to pursue the highest possible goal.
- **One Value**: the application of our achievements to help others so that we do not become self-centered.
- **One Victory**: the knowledge that success leads to further success and winning becomes a habit.

This philosophy applies not only to martial arts but also to daily life. I want you all to be winners in your life and enjoy many successes. Through the application of the "**three V's**," one can realize the true meaning of the martial arts—peace.

Chapter One

The afternoon was bright and sunny. But inside a tall, hollow tree in the middle of the park, a little squirrel could only see the huge world through small holes in her tree-house and feel the warmth of the sun as it melted into the entrance of the house. Cookie, more than her brother and sister, longed to leave the house and venture out of their tree.

Ever since Cookie started talking, she would beg Mother to let her go outside, but Mother would not allow it, because Cookie, her brother and her sister were all still too young. Cookie believed that she was smart enough and strong enough to be able to handle any dangers. Cookie's desire to leave the tree-house caused Mother great stress. Mother knew that Cookie was no ordinary squirrel. Ever since she was born she exhibited a lot of energy and determination. Compared to her brother and sister, Cookie was smarter and more outgoing. She was also very curious, always asking how and why about everything.

When Cookie played with her brother and sister, she felt the tree-house was so tiny compared to the vast forest outside. Outside they would be able to run, jump, and hide. So, Cookie spent hours every day trying to convince Mother to let her go outside. However, Mother knew that when her baby squirrels went out it would have to be when they could protect themselves from the dangers of the forest. So instead of going on adventures beyond the tree-house, Cookie would listen eagerly to the stories that her mother and father told about the outside world. In those stories, Mother and Father continuously warned them about enemies of the forest, especially the hawk.

Cookie began to debate with her mother over the many reasons she should be allowed to go outside. Mother shook her head and said, "The hawk is a squirrel's most dangerous enemy. It usually circles quietly in the air, watching for its prey. Then the hawk swoops down, with lightning speed, to dig its claws into its next meal." Mother always shivered when she talked about the hawk.

Cookie remembered the many times Father complained about the hawk. Father went out each day at sunrise to gather food for the whole family. Sometimes he didn't come home until very late because the enemy hawk would watch their tree to try and catch him. So he had to hide and wait until the hawk left the area, which sometimes took hours.

Father added, "Owls usually hunt at night. Dogs and cats don't usually eat squirrels, but they like to catch them. Dogs can run fast, but they don't climb trees as well as squirrels. Cats are a headache because they can climb trees. They can sit, wait, and watch like a thief for us to pass by. Humans themselves are pretty harmless, but their cars and motorcycles are faster than any other enemy. You need to learn to sense the vibrations and the sounds of the cars and motorcycles."

Father started shaking Cookie's arms and making loud growling noises. "They breathe very loudly, so you must stay away from noisy areas. Cars usually hunt on the roads, but motorcycles can come after you on dirt, grass, and even in the forest. Once those monsters are heading towards you it's too late." He grabbed her again and screamed, "Rraaughh!" Cookie giggled.

"All right, all right, that's enough for tonight." Mother gave Father a mean look and then smiled at Cookie. "You'd better get to sleep. Your brother and sister have already gone to sleep." Cookie pouted, but Mother kissed her on the head and pushed her towards the hole where her brother and sister were sleeping.

That night Cookie dreamed that she was soaring in the sky without any effort. In her dream, she met all the enemies that Mother and Father had warned her about, but they did not try to hurt her. They all smiled, waved, and greeted her by name. "Hello, Cookie. Cooooooookie. Cooooooookie." Even several cars passed over her body, but it didn't hurt. It felt soft, like her sister was rolling over on her. Through the clouds she soared again. Nothing could hurt her. She was Super Squirrel. When she woke up the next morning, she believed that the world was made and existed only for her.

So after lunch, while Mother was napping, Cookie decided to sneak out of the house. Cookie knew that she had to be very quiet to not wake Mother. It was thrilling to tiptoe right past Mother to the entrance. Cookie didn't make a sound. When her brother and sister stopped playing to watch her, Cookie put her finger to her mouth to tell them to be quiet. Near the house entrance, she looked back one last time to make sure Mother was still asleep, and she was.

Cookie stepped up to the edge of the entranceway and looked at the outside world. The wind brushed through Cookie's fur. It was more beautiful than she had imagined. White clouds drifted across a blue sky. The forest was painted green. It was wonderful to finally see the outside world. Cookie's heart raced. She wanted to see it all a little closer. Just as Cookie turned to climb down from the house, a hand grabbed her by the back of her neck.

"WHAT ARE YOU DOING?!" Mother screamed hysterically.

That night, Cookie went to sleep without dinner as punishment. Cookie heard her stomach make growling, hungry noises all night, but she didn't complain. She knew Mother was very furious.

The next morning at breakfast, Mother patted her

head and said, "I love you, Cookie. Please do not try to do that again. You could have been killed. When I believe you are ready we will all go out. When you grow up and become a mother you will understand my punishment. Can you promise me that you will never do that again?"

Cookie nodded her head. "I promise. I'm sorry, Mama."

Mother sighed, "There are a lot of enemies outside waiting to kill us. You have to learn to use your senses. Your father already warned you about staying away from loud, noisy areas, but sometimes when it's quiet that can be a sign of danger, too. Every few seconds you have to look around, even if you think no one is there."

She pulled Cookie into her lap and spoke softly, "You have to learn how to hold your breath and pulse."

Cookie looked confused. "Mama, how can I hold my pulse?"

As she stroked Cookie's head with tender hands, Mother tried to explain. "Well, when you hold your pulse you must first be very still and quiet until you can only hear the sound of your heartbeat. Then you must try to silence even your heartbeat. When there is total silence, you will be able to hear everything around, but nothing will be able to hear you. As you grow you will understand. This is how your father and I survive every day outside."

She hugged Cookie tight. "Now, go play with your brother and sister while I get lunch ready."

Days went by. Cookie did not complain about the small tree-house and she didn't dare ask about going outside. She even stopped asking Father to tell her stories about the hawk and owl when he got home at night. Cookie wasn't going to take any chances at making Mother upset again.

Father had come home early from gathering food that day because it was starting to rain. He brought piles of leaves and sticks. By nightfall, the thunder and lightning were fierce. Cookie's parents tried to cover the entranceway with leaves and sticks, but the wind was too strong. The heavy gusts brought the cold rain into the house.

Cookie shivered in the corner while trying to shelter her brother and sister from the rain with a small leaf. Cookie's parents continued unsuccessfully to try and cover the entrance and block the rain. The entire house and Cookie's family were drenched by the time the storm subsided early the next morning.

When Cookie woke up the next morning, her body ached for more sleep. Her fur was still damp. The rest of her family was still asleep from the long night. Cookie looked out one of the small holes in the tree to see the sun glistening off the wet leaves. As she watched birds glide through the forest, she heard her sister sneeze. The sneeze startled Mother awake. Cookie sat down next to her shivering sister as Mother stroked Sister's feverish head.

Cookie and her brother spent the rest of the day trying to clean and dry the house. They swept the extra water out with the leaves their father brought home the day before. Father reluctantly left the house to gather food for the family while Mother was taking care of Sister, who was very sick. Except for her chores, Cookie stayed next to her sister to help Mother. Over the next few days, Sister got even worse.

Sister knew she wouldn't have too much time with her family. So before Sister fell asleep that night, she asked Mother if the whole family could go out together tomorrow to see the world. Sister hoped Cookie would like this suggestion. Sadly, Mother and Father agreed. They had hoped that their children's first time outside would be filled with fun and anticipation, but the family knew Sister wasn't getting better. This could be her only chance to see the world outside.

Cookie awoke earlier than usual the next day. By the time the rest of the family woke up, she was bursting with excitement. When they climbed down from the tree-house, Cookie carefully helped Sister down to the ground. The earth was full of color and sound. It looked totally different than the view Cookie had from the small window in the tree-house. There were strange bugs, small birds, and colorful flowers that smelled sweet.

Father softly rubbed Sister's head. "You have to understand each bird's song. Sometimes birds sing warnings of danger. Even baby birds are hushed when enemies are hiding or watching." He pointed to a bird's nest in the bushes.

Mother whispered in Cookie's ear, "Be aware of the

wind's directions and the scents they bring. Smell the different flowers and plants. Try to recognize the differences between our scent and other enemy animal scents. Remember all these scents. When Father goes all around gathering food, knowing these scents gives him directions to come home and warns him of nearby enemies."

Cookie hopped to a bright red flower and took a big sniff. The pollen tickled her nose and made her sneeze. Her sister and brother giggled. Cookie laughed and smiled at Mother, but Mother wasn't smiling. A look of terror was on Mother's face. Father was petrified.

"RUN!" Mother was screaming and pointing up in the air.

"HIDE!" Mother and Father instinctively ran into a small bush.

Cookie was faster than her brother and sister. She dove into the bush. Her brother was close behind her. When Cookie saw her sister struggling, she ran back out to help her. Just as she reached Sister, Cookie felt her body being jerked and lifted into the air.

She was flying through the air like in her dream, but she could see the claws and feel the grip around her body tighten. She realized that the hawk had grabbed her.

Cookie shouted, "Leave me alone! Please let me go. My family is waiting for me."

She began to feel dizzy. Everything was going by so fast. Cookie suddenly realized she was a lot higher than her tree-house. She felt faint. She knew that once the hawk landed she would be killed. This was her last chance.

Instead of screaming and begging, Cookie began to struggle and wrestle with the hawk. Its claws began to tighten again. It was getting harder for Cookie to breathe.

She scratched the hawk's legs and sank her teeth into one of its claws. The hawk began to panic. It tried to kill Cookie with a stab of its beak but missed her. When the hawk pecked again, it gashed Cookie's shoulder and neck. Never in her life had Cookie felt that kind of pain. Cookie screamed and began flailing her hands and feet. As the hawk tried to peck again, Cookie's feet accidentally cut the hawk's eye. Instantly, its claws opened. Cookie was free.

The air whipped through Cookie's fur as she fell. Cookie became dizzy again. She felt like she was falling for hours even though only seconds had passed. Cookie could see a building speeding towards her.

She began screaming, "AUGGHH!" Cookie knew the crash was going to kill her. A shadow passed over Cookie. It was the hawk.

The hawk was very angry. It turned and aimed at Cookie. When the hawk's claw reached to grab Cookie's body, it missed. Its eye was injured and still in pain and that made the hawk misjudge the distance. Cookie's body stiffened and her eyes widened as she watched the building get closer and closer. She didn't even notice that the hawk turned to aim for her again.

In the same instant that Cookie threw her arm over

her face to prepare for impact, she felt a hard blow to her back. Instead of grabbing Cookie, the hawk hit her body. Cookie was deflected into a bush a few feet from the building. Her body fell through the bushes, rolled down the small hill, and under a dumpster.

The hawk desperately looked for Cookie inch by inch on the ground. It figured Cookie was dead but couldn't spot her body. The hawk's eye was bleeding badly now. After circling several times, the hawk saw a human walking towards the dumpster. The hawk knew it would have to give up finding Cookie's body. It would have to find breakfast somewhere else. The hawk flew back to the forest clenching its claws. Cookie lay unconscious.

The dumpster was behind an old strip shopping center. The dumpster always smelled strong with old oils, breads, meats, fish, fruits, and vegetables. Most of the businesses in the shopping center were small, and business was slow. There was a karate school, a barbershop, a nail salon, a little grocery store, a repair shop, and a Greek restaurant.

During most of the year, some businesses like the karate school often left their backdoors open for fresh air. The Greek restaurant's backdoor, near the dumpster, was always open because of the heat from the kitchen. Even in the winter, unless it was frigid, they left the door open. Employees who worked at the restaurant sometimes came out from the kitchen to get fresh air and take a small break. They stretched their legs and killed time by walking around in the parking lot in front of the bushes.

The restaurant stayed open later than any of the other businesses. After they served late dinner, they had to clean the kitchen, wash dishes, and reset the tables for the next day. Sometimes employees did not leave until after midnight, depending on the customers. Each night before they left work, the employees threw the trash into the dumpsters, otherwise the pests and bugs would become active within the restaurant. Mr. Gyro, the restaurant owner, was the last to leave and locked up each night.

Mr. Gyro's restaurant was the oldest business in the shopping center. He rented that space since the shopping center was built. When he first opened his restaurant, it was popular and business was good. The food was delicious, the kitchen was spotless, and he and his wife were full of energy to serve the customers. At that time, this building was in the far west end of the city, so everybody enjoyed eating at his restaurant. However, now there were hundreds of bigger, nicer restaurants in the west end, even nationwide restaurant chains.

With all the competition, business was slow and Mr. Gyro was getting old. And ever since Mr. Gyro's wife died, he'd lost his enthusiasm and passion for the business. Everything he did was a repetition of yesterday. His homemade bread tasted like yesterday's bread, his pizza tasted like yesterday's pizza, and his pasta tasted like yesterday's pasta. Nothing changed.

Mr. Gyro thought about retiring several times, but

what else would he do? This had become a habit. He even spoke to his son about taking over the restaurant, but his son didn't want to take over the business. So after Mr. Gyro's son finished college, he moved to New York.

Mr. Gyro's son didn't want to live in this small town because he enjoyed the big city life of New York. His son didn't want to be involved in the restaurant business because it meant dedicating seven days a week, from early morning to late night, and this meant less time for himself. Mr. Gyro's son told him that he never enjoyed being the only child of parents who owned a restaurant because they barely spent time with him when he needed them.

Mr. Gyro's son told him, "This town is too slow for me. I'd rather work in the fast-paced city. And in an office I'd have vacation time, sick leave, benefits, and the possibility of promotion and raises. Someday, if I'm doing well, I could be CEO of the company. But if I run the restaurant, there is no guarantee that the restaurant will be as successful as during your time because at that time you didn't have as much competition. When you first opened, your equipment was new, your building was new, and everyone could remember your name and food. But now there is so much competition. The competition could be some stockholder in a big chain restaurant or somebody in Alaska who has oil money. I know you raised me comfortably and educated me well, but as you know your assets are not near enough to run a successful restaurant."

After talking with his son, Mr. Gyro's energy and will power were even lower.

Mr. Gyro's restaurant was not as secure as in the past. In the restaurant business, owners must keep the backdoor locked at all times to control employee theft. So when employees parked behind the shopping center, they would have to walk around to the front door. Mr. Gyro knew that a bad employee who wanted to steal could put food and supplies in bags in the dumpsters or directly in the trunk of their car. Knowing all this, Mr. Gyro still allowed the backdoor to be unlocked.

Mr. Gyro knew that leaving the back doorunlocked was risky, but he didn't care and he trusted his employees. The employees could come and go through the backdoor anytime. Mr. Gyro even installed a screen door for when the door was left open. The screen prevented bugs and flies from entering, but it didn't prevent everything from getting into his restaurant.

Mr. Gyro didn't realize he was also taking care of several families of mice in his old attic ceiling, that connected to all the other businesses in the shopping center. The mice had lived in the attic since the shopping center was built. While Mr. Gyro's wife was alive, she often put down poison to kill them, but these mouse families continued to survive from generation to generation.

There was a loud, rumbling noise. Cookie awoke startled to see a dumpster above her head. As she tried to comprehend what had happened, the memories of her family, her sister, the hawk, and the bush came flooding back. Cookie realized her parents were not there and neither were her brother or sister. She was alone under the smelly dumpster with a dull, throbbing pain in her whole body, especially her bloody shoulder and neck. Cookie continued to drift in and out of consciousness.

She had no energy to move. It was difficult to breathe because her neck was in a lot of pain. She tried to breathe as softly and slowly as possible, otherwise the pain was so severe she would have to hold her breath. She continuously tried to inhale and exhale slowly. Exhaling was much easier than inhaling. She did not know how much more she could take. She did not know whether it was day or night, or whether she would live or die.

This summer it hadn't rained often, but fortunately for Cookie it was not dry either. Rain ran down from the bushes, under the dumpster, and into the parking lot. Cookie licked up the rain unconsciously. This helped her breathe steadily again. She got more than she needed, but she was still unable to move at all. She realized that if she gave up now she would die soon. She began to realize that she hadn't moved for a long time. So Cookie began to slowly and gently move each part of her body. She wiggled her toes, circled her ankles, bent her knees, shifted her hips, wiggled her fingers, flexed her elbows, and rolled her shoulders. Any attempt to move her right fingers, arm, or shoulder caused her terrible pain.

As the rain fell harder, Cookie began to feel cold and achy in her shoulder and neck. She knew she would have to crawl out of this place because the running water was beginning to rise in the parking lot and she might drown. Cookie tried to turn over on her stomach, but the pain in her shoulder and neck was too intense. She could now feel the throbbing of her heartbeat in her shoulder. She realized she would not be able to use her right arm.

Cookie remembered her mother telling her bedtime stories about squirrels that didn't have tails because owls would catch their tails. When other squirrels teased the tailless squirrels, they were never embarrassed, because they had survived the owl. Life was hard for those tailless squirrels. They had to work twice as hard as the other squirrels to maintain their balance, coordination, and speed. But with hard work, they were able to do everything the other squirrels could do. After her bedtime story, Mother would say, "Always do your best every single second to survive."

Cookie knew she had no choice but to move or drown. She knew she could stay here and die comfortably by drowning, but she chose to live. When she turned over onto her stomach, the throbbing in her shoulder and neck turned into a sharp, stabbing pain. Cookie decided to use her legs and tail to push herself slowly from under the dumpster. She twisted her hips and legs while her left hand tightly held her right shoulder. The pain was becoming unbearable, but she had to keep moving. She pushed again, again, again.

Finally, she pushed out from under the dumpster.

The rain beat down on Cookie's tiny body, washing the blood from her fur. She could not see clearly in the dark, heavy rain. She did not know where to go or how to avoid the rain. She did not know how to gather food or fix her shoulder and neck. She did not know where she was or how to find her family. She knew she couldn't climb a tree because of her shoulder. Tears began to mix with the rain on Cookie's cheeks.

She wanted to cry out loud so that her family might hear her and save her, but she remembered that Mother once said, *"Do not make noise just anywhere. When you are in the house you can do whatever you want. You can laugh, play, shout, and do anything, even cry. But when you make noise outside, you put your life in danger."* Cookie's tears fell in silence.

Cookie lifted her head and spotted some small bushes behind the dumpster. She pushed herself up the small hill and under a bush. The pain was now excruciating. Cookie slipped in and out of consciousness as memories of her family, the hawk, and the dumpster overwhelmed her aching head until she passed out under the bush.

Chapter Two

The next morning, warm sunlight showered Cookie's wet body under the bush. As she slept, she looked like a peaceful, happy little squirrel. Cookie didn't realize that there were two bright, sparkling eyes focused on her. These eyes skimmed over her head to her tail. The curious eyes belonged to Andy, one of the mice who lived in Mr. Gyro's attic.

Andy was the most unusual mouse in his family. He was adventurous, courageous, and brave, but he also had a kind, gentle heart. Part of his left ear had been ripped off a few months ago in a fight with another mouse.

When Andy noticed the blood around Cookie's shoulder, he felt sorry for her, but there was nothing he could do. Andy knew that life was not fair for everybody. Andy knew if he were in the wrong place at the wrong time, even he wouldn't be able to survive. He didn't know what was beyond death, but he knew that dying was a scary thing, especially when you might end up someone's dinner.

Andy could tell that he was a lot older than Cookie. She looked like a baby squirrel. Even so, Andy was a lot smaller than her. Andy knew that he should not get involved in someone else's trouble. That's how he was taught. Unless their food supply was the issue, it was not their concern. All mice thought this way. But Andy always thought that food should not be the only reason to live. He thought, *Eat to live, not live to eat.*

Andy scratched the ground to make noise to get Cookie's attention, but there was no response. Andy ran closer to the bush, picked up a small rock from near the bush, and ran back to keep a safe distance. When you do not know your opponent it is better to keep a cautious distance in order to run if needed. Andy threw the rock into the bush near Cookie, but she still did not respond.

Andy knew he had to get closer. He picked up a small twig and tapped Cookie's foot. When Cookie blinked, she saw two twinkling eyes and a big smile looking back at her. Cookie was so startled that she forgot her pain and tried to crawl away. Her right arm collapsed numb under her. Cookie pushed herself down the small hill and under the dumpster again. It was the only place she knew to hide. Cookie watched Andy carefully and realized that he was not trying to harm or attack her, but she did not trust him.

Andy followed slowly at a distance behind Cookie.

He could tell she was very frightened. Andy watched her struggle and felt really sorry for her. He was upset with himself because he woke her up for nothing.

That night back in Andy's attic, he said nothing to his family about the baby squirrel he saw. He ate quickly and went to sleep with his belly full. Andy tossed and turned all night. Something bothered him. The image of the wounded baby squirrel crowded his mind. He knew she wouldn't survive there. It was only a matter of time.

Andy knew that his selfish curiosity awakened the squirrel. He only wanted to know if she was dead or alive. Andy rubbed his left ear. He remembered the pain he felt when he injured his ear. He was lucky to have his whole family there to watch out for him, feed him, and comfort him.

Andy knew that the dumpster had plenty of food in it, but the squirrel's injuries made it impossible for her to crawl in and out. Also the bush area was safe, but the squirrel would not be able to crawl up a tree. Andy reassured himself that the small space under the dumpster's lift was safe from cats, dogs, or other predators.

Andy still could not sleep comfortably. He knew that for safety purposes, mice did not go out at night unless they did not find enough food earlier. Andy sat up. "Why should I wait until tomorrow morning?" He decided to take a chance. If the baby squirrel was still under the dumpster it would be a sign for him to help her. Andy gathered some food together and quietly crawled out of the attic.

The stars were shining around a full moon, crickets were chirping, and lightning bugs were playing near the bushes. Andy watched carefully to make sure the coast was clear. He was not sure if the baby squirrel would still be there. When Andy was sure that everything was all right, he ran to the dumpster. The baby squirrel was sleeping quietly.

Andy kneeled down next to her. He touched her leg and whispered, "Are you all right?"

Cookie opened her eyes slowly. She was too tired to try and get away again.

Andy could see she was very weak. Holding up a small piece of bread, he said, "I brought you some food."

Cookie didn't say anything because she couldn't understand Andy's mouse language. But when Cookie saw Andy holding the bread out to her she understood what Andy was trying to say and she accepted the bread.

The food was so delicious to Cookie. She hadn't eaten in what seemed to be so many days. She swallowed the food in large pieces without chewing because she was so hungry.

While Cookie inhaled her food she watched Andy closely. Andy was a tiny but strong-looking mouse. She could see that a small piece of his left ear was ripped off. His eyes were alert and shiny.

Cookie tried to tell Andy that she appreciated the food. Andy couldn't understand what she was saying but understood what she meant.

Over the next several days, Andy was very busy. He had to gather extra food for Cookie. As Cookie became stronger she ate more than Andy. Andy spent all his time with Cookie. Cookie quickly learned Andy's language because she was a smart baby and tried hard.

During their time together, Andy told Cookie about his twin brother—Ronnie, his family, their neighbors, and their attic above the Greek restaurant in the shopping center. Cookie told Andy about her family, her sick sister, and her wonderful tree-house. Cookie did not know where her family was, whether her poor sister was dead from her illness, or how to find her way home. And when she thought about the enemy hawk she couldn't breathe. That hawk still horrified her. Tears rolled down her cheeks without a whimper.

Andy was very sympathetic to Cookie's situation and what had happened to her. He promised Cookie that he would help her until she was well enough to find her family.

Andy was so busy running in and out that his family was worried that he might be up to no good. As Andy gulped down his dinner as usual, his dad watched him intently. "Son, are you in trouble? Why are you so busy? Are you going to have the other ear ripped off too? Is that what you want?"

"No, I don't think so," Andy answered mechanically as if not really listening. "I'm just helping somebody. There is a poor baby squirrel wounded under the dumpster. I'm just helping her out." In between his bites of food, Andy explained Cookie's situation.

"Son, if I were you I would stay out of it. That squirrel must learn her own way. Besides, squirrels can eat us if they are really hungry, because they are bigger and stronger than us."

Andy finally stopped eating to look up. "Dad, if I was in her situation and I had lost my family and she was helping me to get strong, she would be a wonderful squirrel. You would probably be grateful for her. Wouldn't you?"

"Son, this is different. Do not argue with me. Let's look at the situation as it is now."

"Dad, that's why we have lived here for generations, our families help each other." Andy had stopped eating completely. "We had the opportunity to move to the new, bigger shopping center, but we only look at the present. Let's think about tomorrow. If this shopping center were gone tomorrow, what would we do? Where would we live? How would we protect ourselves from predators? In the new shopping center Mr. Max's families have plenty of food and plenty of space. They can raise so many families. We have limited families because we don't have enough space."

"Son, I understand what you are saying, but do you know why you are so smart? It is because of this shopping center. That's part of the reason. I think you are the smartest mouse in our family and community. Do you know why?"

Andy sighed, "You have told me a hundred times already. I'm tired of hearing that story. Please stop. I want to help Cookie. She really needs my help. If I turn my back on her, she will surely die."

"Son, I worry about your safety, especially around the dumpster area. Sometimes there are wild cats waiting for us."

Andy's mom and little sister shivered and looked at each other.

Andy's dad leaned in towards the family to talk softly, "Several members of the mouse families here were killed by those cats before you were born. We haven't seen the cats lately, but they can show up anytime."

The whole family sat quietly for a few minutes. Suddenly Andy jumped to his feet, bursting with excitement. "Dad, why don't we bring her inside our house? Let her stay with us until she is better."

"No way!" shouted Ronnie. Until now, Andy's twin brother had been indifferent to the conversation. Ronnie turned to his dad. "Andy is confused. It is too dangerous to bring that squirrel into our house."

Andy's dad nodded his head. "I agree. You can't bring a stranger in our house. Headaches always come up sooner or later. Anyway, I'm warning you, Andy. Leave this matter alone and allow it to take care of itself."

Ronnie glanced at Andy with a twisted smile and guffawed. "Excellent decision, Dad!"

That night Andy couldn't sleep. He was busy wondering, *How will I get Cookie into our house?* Then he remembered that the attic above the martial arts school was vacant.

That attic had been empty ever since Vicky got married to Spence. Vicky's family hated living above the martial arts school, so when Spence offered her entire family a new home in the new, bigger shopping center they moved out. The martial arts school was so noisy. There was unexpected screaming and yelling. And when they hit punching bags the vibrations shook the entire attic. Ever since Vicky's family moved out, no one wanted to live in that attic.

Andy never wanted to accept Vicky's marriage to Spence. Spence was selfish and mean. Spence always bragged about how he was strong, tough and cunning. Spence always carried a shiny steel needle as his weapon. He used it for protection and to show off or to scare others. Andy did not like Spence's arrogance.

Andy missed Vicky. She was so cute and adorable. But he didn't want to think about Ronnie's ex-fiancée at all. Andy had feelings for Vicky too, but she was in love with Ronnie. At one time, Andy thought that Ronnie and Vicky would get married. When his dad realized that both his sons were in love with Vicky, he demanded that they end their relationship with Vicky immediately. His dad believed that brotherhood was more important than a girl. That's why his dad encouraged Vicky's father to allow the marriage to Spence.

Andy shook his head and thought again of the empty attic. He decided that Vicky's old home would be the safest place for Cookie to live. Now came the problem—how could Cookie get into the attic?

He knew that Cookie could not climb up the building's wall by herself. Even with Andy's help it was almost impossible. Andy tried to figure out how Cookie could climb up without using her injured arm. He thought all night. How, how, how?

Then Andy had an idea. If Cookie could hold his tail in her mouth and use one arm and her legs to climb while Andy climbed, he could help pull her up with his tail. All they had to do was synchronize their steps.

Andy's heart was pumping fast. He was excited about his plan. Andy couldn't wait until tomorrow, so he ran out immediately to tell Cookie. When he reached the entrance of the attic, Andy could see the dim light of the rising sun. He had been up all night.

Cookie thought Andy's plan was impossible. And after Andy told her about his family's disapproval, she was so discouraged she didn't even want to try. Andy asked Cookie to at least try a little.

While Cookie practiced crawling on the ground, Andy watched cautiously for danger. As Cookie crawled, her right arm dragged lifelessly on the ground. Her right arm had no strength and was numb.

Then they practiced together to get their footsteps in sync. Practice went a lot better than Cookie thought it would. Except for eating breaks, they worked all day. Cookie was exhausted, but they were both excited about the plan now. Cookie agreed to practice on the wall tomorrow.

After Andy left, Cookie quietly slipped out by herself and practiced crawling around the parking lot and the dumpster. She was cautious to listen and watch for enemies.

Cookie knew getting to the attic was the only way she could survive. There was no other choice. She was so tired her legs trembled, but she felt a strange strength coming from her lower stomach. She began to focus on her breathing.

Ever since she first awoke under the dumpsters, unable to move or breathe freely, she had tried to control her physical pain in her neck and shoulder by controlling her breathing. Her slow, soft breathing automatically made her more aware of her lower stomach.

Focused on her deep stomach breathing, Cookie slipped back under the dumpster. Her deep breathing had become a habit. As Cookie fell into the deepest sleep ever, the sun began to rise.

All morning long Andy and Cookie practiced climbing on the wall together. It wasn't easy. The problem was that Cookie's left hand alone could not balance her as she climbed the wall. Every time she tried to take her feet off the ground to scale the wall, she would lose her balance and fall back down. And each time Cookie fell, it was with a hard, painful thud that made her wince. Cookie cried without making any noise. One hand's grip was not enough to hold up her body. Even holding Andy's tail, they continued to sway, which would cause them both to fall down after a few feet.

After dozens of attempts, both were able to at least

land on their feet as they fell instead of on their heads. As they sensed that they were beginning to lose their balance they learned to voluntarily jump down with a proper two-foot landing. After they learned this falling technique, they began to laugh each time they landed instead of becoming discouraged. They tried again and again, giggling each time they landed.

There was a hole in the wall where all the shops' telephone cables entered the building. This was the entrance into Andy's home and the shopping center's attic. Cookie and Andy couldn't find any area of scratched and damaged wall to improve their grip that went all the way up to the entrance. It was an old brick building, but a single-handed grip was impossible for crawling up vertically all the way to the entrance.

While Andy and Cookie were resting and having dinner together under the dumpster, they heard a noise in the parking lot. They saw a ladder being placed against the martial arts school rooftop. Two men, dressed in all white, climbed the ladder to the roof with tools.

Andy knew the rooftop had a lot of machines that made loud, scary noises. Sometimes humans would go up on the rooftops on the other shops as well. Andy whispered to Cookie, "There is also a way to get into the attic on the roof. There are many vents on the roof, but only one of the vents is the secret entrance. All other vents are traps that can kill."

Cookie thought the ladder appeared much easier than trying to climb up the wall. The ladder was not as steep as the wall of the building. Cookie studied the ladder carefully. Hopping or climbing up the steps would be difficult with one arm. Ascending the sides of the ladder seemed easier. Cookie watched the men move back and forth on the roof. A few minutes later, the two men climbed down and went back into the building with the tools and the ladder.

Cookie and Andy looked at each other. Both of them thought they should have taken a chance on the stepladder today. Andy didn't know when they would or if they would get another chance.

Early the next morning, while Cookie was waiting to meet Andy for breakfast, the backdoor to the martial arts school opened and a man came out with the stepladder. The man leaned the ladder against the building and climbed up to the rooftop.

Cookie's heart was pounding. She knew she had to try, but Andy was not there. Cookie hesitated and thought, *Should I wait until Andy comes? Is there any place I can hide or any food on the roof? How will Andy find me?*

Worry filled Cookie from her head to her toes. She knew she had to do it. She needed a permanent place to hide until she was completely well.

As she moved closer to the stepladder, she could feel her heart beating in her chest. Once she got to the side railing of the ladder, she began to quickly crawl up. It was much easier than crawling up the wall but still difficult with one hand. Cookie wished Andy was there to see her.

When she reached the rooftop and pulled herself

onto the ledge, she noticed that the man was looking down at her. Cookie froze. She was frightened and scared. The man just chuckled and smiled at her. The man walked right by Cookie and climbed back down the ladder. Cookie saw the top of the ladder disappear from the ledge and a few seconds later heard the backdoor close.

Andy was surprised to find Cookie's space under the dumpster deserted. He began looking for Cookie. He looked around the entire dumpster and in the bushes but couldn't find her anywhere. Andy began to imagine the worst. Could the wild cat his dad had spoken of taken Cookie or did the enemy hawk come back for revenge?

Andy scolded himself, "I should have persuaded my family to help me bring Cookie inside. I should not have left her alone last night. I should have told Cookie to climb the ladder yesterday."

Andy searched for hours, running around the dumpster and into the bushes over and over. He couldn't forget Cookie's tearful eyes when they first met. Andy thought, *Just yesterday, Cookie was so happy as she tried to climb the scratched wall a few feet. She was so excited and enthusiastic.* Andy realized his cheeks were wet. He sat down under the dumpster with his face in his hands.

Cookie immediately realized that the rooftop was a lot hotter than under the dumpster. Her feet were almost burning. The tar on the rooftop was sticky and hot. She could smell the tar smoldering under the blazing sun. Cookie needed to move into a shaded area as soon as possible; otherwise she was going to faint.

There were no trees or bushes on the rooftop. The only place she could go was next to a machine, but it made loud noises and blew hot air. Cookie saw many different-sized and -shaped vents all around the rooftop.

She remembered Andy telling her about another way into the attic. The secret entrance was through a vent. She looked at all the vents again. It was too hot to explore the roof now. Cookie crawled next to the largest vent and crouched down in its shade. After a minute or two, her feet felt better. She decided to wait in the shade until dark.

Cookie was hungry and thirsty. She realized that there was no food, no water, no way down, and no Andy to show her the secret entrance. Cookie knew that if she jumped down from the building to get back to the dumpster she would break every bone in her body. She was trapped.

Cookie began to realize how wonderful Andy was. He always brought wet bread so Cookie did not need water, he would massage her numb fingers, and he always encouraged her. Now Cookie was alone, and she didn't know how she was going to stay alive.

Chapter Three

When Andy woke up it was dark and he was still under the dumpster. Cookie never showed up. Andy knew that something bad must have happened to Cookie, but he didn't want to believe it.

He had hoped that when Cookie got well he would help her find her family. He felt guilty about not warning her more about the dangers of this area. She was bigger than him, but she was very young. She did not have good judgment.

Andy felt the blood drain from his face. His mind was empty and his heart ached, but he knew he had to get home. His family would worry about him. Andy rushed across the parking lot, up the wall, and into the telephone cable entrance.

Using the light of the full moon, Cookie decided to examine the vents and look for the secret entrance. The rooftop was much cooler and easier to walk on. She walked around the rooftop, inch by inch, investigating each vent carefully.

She heard grinding noises from some of the vents, warm air blew out of many, and one vent sounded like humans. Some of the vents smelled delicious and some smelled like the dumpster. Cookie tried to look inside the vents, but she could not see anything. It was too dark.

She knew Andy wouldn't lie to her. She used her nose to try and sniff for any mouse scents to follow, but the tar smell was still too strong. Cookie was beginning to get nervous. She began to tremble. Cookie could not shout or call to Andy, because she had to be quiet. She knew an enemy might hear her.

As Cookie looked around the rooftop at the vents, she noticed the vents were reflecting in the moonlight. All the vents were new and shiny, except one.

When Andy came into the entranceway of his home, his twin brother, Ronnie, was on his way out. Ronnie growled, "Because you were out playing all day, I have to do your job and go back out to find more dinner for the family." Ronnie pushed past Andy and out the entrance.

As the two oldest and only sons, it was Andy's and Ronnie's job to collect food for the family each day while their mom and dad stayed home to watch their little sister, Sissy. Sissy was too young to go outside and gather food.

Andy stood dazed. He had not eaten all day. He had waited all day for Cookie under the dumpster. He had not done his chores and now his whole family was eating dinner late because he hadn't gotten food for them.

Cookie looked at the old, rusty vent. She could still hear humans shouting. The vent was covered with dust and cobwebs. Cookie's instincts told her that if she had to choose a secret entrance this old one would be it.

But how could she be sure? She remembered Andy saying, *"There are many vents on the roof, but only one of the vents is the secret entrance. All other vents are traps that can KILL."* She couldn't convince herself to go in the vent.

She decided to go to the ledge of the shopping center rooftop to watch for Andy. After what seemed like forever, Cookie saw a mouse running to the bushes from the shopping center. He looked like Andy, but his ear was not ripped.

Without concern about enemies, Cookie shouted, "Hey, I'm looking for Andy. Do you know him?"

The mouse stopped and looked up toward the ledge. "Yep. Who are you?"

"My name is Cookie. I am Andy's friend. I need his help. Can you tell him I'm here?"

"How in the world can a squirrel be a friend to a mouse? Don't make me laugh." Then without looking at her again, Ronnie ran into the bushes.

Cookie waited for that mouse to come back from the bush for a long time, but she couldn't spot him anywhere. Andy never showed up either. Cookie knew that for safety purposes, she could not sit out in the open on the ledge all night. Heavy hearted, Cookie went back to wait under the largest vent.

Andy tried to explain why he missed his chores as his dad reminded him that his responsibility should first be to his family. Andy was too tired and too hungry to argue his point of view.

As Andy and his family gathered for a late dinner, Ronnie scoffed, "Where were you all day? Meeting a new girlfriend?"

Andy shot Ronnie a hateful look but then put his head down and ate quietly. Andy's thoughts were only of Cookie.

As Andy swallowed his food, he wondered if Cookie was hungry. He knew she couldn't find food on her own. Andy hoped that she was somewhere safe. Maybe she had gone deeper into the forest and was lost. Tomorrow he would begin looking for her again.

Ronnie watched Andy maliciously. Ronnie never mentioned seeing Cookie on the rooftop. He knew if he didn't say anything Cookie would die up there soon. He tried to rationalize his silence by telling himself, "She was going to die sooner or later anyway." Ronnie still resented his brother for the trouble he caused in his engagement to Vicky.

Cookie knew she had to make up her mind. She went back to the edge to look for the mouse or Andy, but she didn't see anything. Cookie felt like the moon was following her as she paced back and forth from the old, rusty vent to the rooftop edge.

Cookie heard wings flapping in the air. When she looked up at the sky, there was an owl flying towards the rooftop. Cookie froze. She couldn't move. It reminded her of the enemy hawk. The owl flew by her and landed on the ledge of the rooftop.

Cookie didn't want to take any chances. She took a deep breath, and without thinking, she ran to the old vent as fast as she could. Cookie put her head into the vent. It was pitch dark inside, but she jumped in anyway.

It felt like she was falling forever, but within seconds she hit the floor with a thud. Cookie had fallen into an enormous open space. It was dim and dusty. She knew instantly that she had chosen the right vent. Cookie sighed with relief. She knew she was safe now. Cookie felt tears fill her eyes. Hungry, tired, and exhausted, she fell asleep with the moonlight shining on her through the vent.

When Cookie woke up, she could see that it was morning. Through the vent the sky was bright and blue. As Cookie looked at the sky, she realized that the vent was unreachable. She stood on her tiptoes and even jumped to reach the vent's hole, but she wasn't even close to reaching the ceiling where it was located.

She decided to look around. Cookie wondered, *How*

will I get food? How do I find Andy? Are there any enemies in here? She explored the attic space step by step without making any noise.

It was a huge place. There was light coming up through a hole in the middle of the attic floor. Cookie crept slowly towards the hole. It had a chain through it that led down to a big red bag. The hole looked just big enough for her to fit through, but Cookie knew it would be hard to climb down the chain with one hand.

Cookie stuck her head through the hole to take a peek. The floor looked soft and padded. She could see windows on the far wall that looked out at the other side of the building. Cookie was surprised when she saw herself in the mirrors covering a side wall. She waved to herself.

Cookie pulled her head out of the hole. She thought she heard something in the attic. When she moved closer to a small opening in the attic wall, she began to hear two mice talking through the walls.

She frantically tried to push herself through the small opening, but she was much too big. Cookie listened again. She thought she recognized that one of the voices belonged to the mouse she saw from the rooftop ledge.

She shouted, "Andy! Andy! I'm here in the attic." No one answered, and the talking stopped. Cookie could smell Andy's scent through the opening. She shouted again, "Andy, I made it! I made it into the attic." There was silence. She shouted again and again until her voice was hoarse. Cookie sat down next to the opening. She knew Andy would come home soon and she would try again.

Ronnie and his dad froze when they heard someone shouting for Andy from Vicky's old house. Ronnie was furious. They both stood still in silence as the shouting voice continued.

Ronnie whispered to his dad, "Andy must have told that squirrel where the secret entrance was. How could Andy share our family secret with a stranger? That squirrel could become our enemy at any time!"

His dad shook his head and whispered back, "Where is Andy now?"

"How should I know? He left early again. He's so busy all the time. He's probably looking for another friend. Maybe this time it'll be an owl or cat. Who knows?"

"Ronnie, go find Andy. Tell him to come home immediately."

Ronnie was fuming as he crawled out of the telephone cable entrance to search for Andy.

Andy's dad was beginning to worry about this new situation. He never thought the secret entrance would be told to another animal. How could he handle this squirrel? He knew that a squirrel could kill a mouse. He surveyed the situation in his mind. Even though the squirrel was wounded now, later when she healed her behavior could change. If he wanted to lead the squirrel out of the building, would it come back again? If he wanted to kill the squirrel, how would he do it? He knew he would have to use the poison that Mrs. Gyro had left in the attic above the restaurant. The last time the poison was used it was to kill a different enemy…the rats.

Years ago, Andy's great-grandfather, Tag, and Mr. Max's grandfather, Wood, were great friends. Tag and Wood both lived in this shopping center with their families for generations. Their families were very close.

One night the grocery store caught fire. Wood's family escaped safely, but the fire destroyed their attic home. Tag invited Wood's family to move in with his family.

The grocery store fire destroyed everything inside, but none of the other businesses were harmed. The humans threw the burned packages and boxes of food into the dumpster along with bottles of burnt vitamins.

The vitamins smelled like smoke but tasted like candy to the mice. Because they were easy to collect and carry back to the attic, the mice ate these burnt vitamins for every meal.

After a few weeks of eating the burnt vitamins, Tag and Wood began to notice a difference in themselves and other mice. The mice were exhibiting intelligence well beyond the average mouse. They knew that their physical strength was limited so they used more judgment. The mice became more resourceful, intuitive, and clever. However, the more intelligent the mice became, the unhappier they became.

Before they took the vitamins, they were content with life. The mice never complained about anything and had no worries. Their only concerns were gathering food and staying safe from predators. When a predator was near, they were scared and alert, but as soon as they were out of danger, they were happy and carefree.

Now the mice were thinking about tomorrow's comfort and safety. They had to prepare and plan ahead of time. Happiness was replaced by anxiety. The wiser they became the more they worried.

Wood began to feel that two families living in the same home didn't provide enough space and privacy. He thought about his descendants' futures too. When the newer, bigger shopping center was built, Wood recognized that the new shopping center was a good place to move to for his family and his descendents.

Wood knew he would have to fight the rats that had already moved in there. The rats were bigger and stronger, but Wood thought he was smarter than the other mice and certainly smarter than any rat. He devised a plan.

Wood and some other family members would sneak over to the new shopping center and put Mrs. Gyro's poison into the rats' water supply. Tag wanted to help with the plan, but Wood was suspicious of Tag's true intentions.

The plan worked. However, Tag did not return with Wood and his family. Wood told his family that Tag had forgotten the details of the plan and accidentally drank the poisoned water. Ever since Tag died, Andy's grandfather and father had forbidden anyone to go near that poison again.

Andy's dad wondered if today, after all those years, he would have to use that poison.

Andy was far from home, looking deep in the forest. He was still looking around for Cookie, but he couldn't spot or smell her anywhere. His shoulders were sagging. He knew he had to give up looking for Cookie. She was gone.

"Andy!" Ronnie was coming over the small hill. "I knew you would be out here looking for something. Dad wants you to come home right now."

Andy ignored his brother and continued looking.

Ronnie grabbed Andy's arm. "If you don't come right now, I will drag you home. Let's go!"

Andy jerked his arm from Ronnie's grasp and turned to continue into the forest.

Ronnie smirked, "Are you looking for that squirrel?"

Andy spun around. "YES! Do you have any idea what happened to her?"

"Maybe," Ronnie teased. "But you've got to come home now."

"If you know something, you had better tell me now or I won't come home with you."

"Dad said to bring you home right now. He is very angry. You made big trouble."

"I don't care what you think. If you think you have the strength, drag me home!"

Ronnie grabbed Andy's arm and began to pull him. Andy shoved Ronnie so hard Ronnie lost his balance on the hill. Ronnie fell down and rolled into a bush.

Ronnie was fuming. When Ronnie got to his feet, he ran up the hill and threw his shoulder into Andy's chest, knocking Andy to the ground hard. Before Andy could stand, a foot stepped on Andy's chest pushing him back to the ground. When Andy looked up he saw Spence and several soldiers standing above him.

Spence laughed. "You are brothers but always fighting like cats and dogs." Spence was slowly putting more of his weight onto Andy's chest. "Didn't I tell you both never to come on this property? This is mine. You don't listen."

Andy struggled under Spence's weighted foot. Ronnie was too terrified to move or speak. Spence looked at Ronnie. "Are you still looking for Vicky? She is mine." Spence motioned his soldiers in closer and looked at Ronnie again. "I'm going to break your legs today so you will not be able to come here again the rest of your life."

As Spence's soldiers tried to grab Ronnie's arm, Ronnie hit one of the soldiers in the face and ran down the hill as fast as he could.

Spence laughed again and yelled after Ronnie, "You coward!"

Spence looked down at Andy, smiled and then kicked Andy in the face. Blood dripped from the corner of Andy's mouth. Andy grabbed Spence's leg and punched him in the groin.

Spence dropped to his knees, gasping for air. He thought he was going to die. Spence pointed at Andy and shouted, "KILL HIM!" Spence's soldiers jumped on Andy instantly. The soldiers punched and kicked Andy without mercy. Andy couldn't shout.

Suddenly Andy felt a sharp pain in his side. It was Spence's needle weapon. In a fit of anger, Spence had gotten to his feet and stabbed Andy in the side with all his strength. As Andy began to gasp for air, the soldiers backed away from Andy, and even Spence looked surprised by his actions.

"STOP IT, STOP IT!" Andy's dad pushed Spence to the ground with all his strength and then bent down to his son. Andy's blood began to soak the ground. Gritting his teeth, Andy's dad looked at Spence. "If my son dies, you die too! I promise you."

Spence stood up. "Old man, your sons started it first. It's not my fault. I warned them not to come into my territory. They were sneaking over here to try to steal my wife!"

Andy's dad clenched his fist and before Spence could react, Andy's dad had gotten to his feet and punched Spence in the face, knocking him on his back. Spence's soldiers jumped on Andy's dad. They began to kick and punch him as they had done to Andy moments earlier.

Spence scoffed, "It's not my fault. Your son started the fight." He wiped his bloody chin with his hands. He gave his soldiers a signal with his eyes to stop beating Andy's dad. Using a leaf, Spence cleaned Andy's blood off his needle weapon and limped away. "Leave them. Let's go." The soldiers followed Spence over the hill.

Andy's dad crawled next to Andy. Andy's breathing was shallow. He knew Andy was not going to make it.

"Dad, I'm sorry for all this trouble," Andy's voice was frail. "I didn't come here looking for Vicky. I was looking for my friend Cookie that I told you about before. Dad, I make nothing but trouble for you. Are you hurt?"

"Son, don't worry. We will both be okay. You are tough and strong." His dad took Andy's hand. "Your friend is in our house, so don't worry about her. Just relax."

"What did you say, Dad? Cookie is in our house?"

"Well, she is in Vicky's old house."

Andy tried to sit up. "How did she get there?"

"Lie down. Lie down." His dad pushed him back to the ground. "Ronnie didn't tell you about that? We think she used our secret entrance on the rooftop to get into the attic."

"I didn't know that. Dad, can you promise me one thing? If I die, can you take care of her? She is all alone. Will you take care of her until she is well so she can go back to find her family? She is very young and she doesn't know how to survive in the world. Will you take care of her for me?"

"Son, don't worry. I want you to relax. Don't talk."

"Dad, can you promise me please?"

"Okay, I promise."

Andy smiled at his dad, closed his eyes, and peacefully took his last breath.

His father held Andy's hand tightly. "Son, I promise you Spence will be punished."

As Ronnie ran up the hill with his mom and little

sister, he found his dad crying over Andy's dead body. Andy looked so peaceful. There was nothing they could do for Andy. Everyone began to weep. Ronnie cried the hardest, because he felt guilty.

Andy's body was getting cold. They knew it was time to leave. His mom picked some leaves off the bushes and laid them over Andy's body. Sissy blew a kiss to Andy. "Goodbye, Andy."

Ronnie helped carry his dad back to the house. Ronnie knew he would never see his twin brother again. Andy was fun, energetic, and smart, but he was gone now. Ronnie's eyes were wet and he began to realize that he was spiteful and small-minded.

When they returned home, Ronnie realized his dad's injuries were more serious than they looked. His mom tried to be calm for Sissy's sake, but the entire family was worried and upset.

Ronnie sat next to his dad and held his hand.

"Ronnie," his dad strained to talk, "I promised Andy that I would take care of Cookie, the squirrel. I want you to remember this. If something happens to me, I need you to take care of her until she gets well. Then she can go to look for her own family. While she is under my roof, I must take care of her. Can you promise this?"

"Dad, I don't think it's a good idea. Cookie caused this trouble for Andy. How can we help her?"

"Ronnie, I promised Andy. It was his last wish. Do you understand? Can you promise me?"

"I will try."

"Ronnie, I don't think I am going to make it. You are the one that will have to lead this family. I want you to think big and act big. Think possible rather than impossible. You know Spence is very strong. We can't compete with his soldiers. If they really wanted to destroy us, they could wipe us out. Cookie may be able to help us. Don't you think so?"

Ronnie looked appalled. "Dad, I can handle Spence without Cookie's help. Besides, she's not even well herself."

"Son, she's injured now. She will get better. Besides, she only has two options, get well and become strong or get worse and die. If she gets worse and dies, there is nothing we can do. But if she gets well, then she can be really helpful to our family. Squirrels have excellent eyesight and they are bigger and stronger than us. I know you blame Cookie for Andy's death, but please, promise me that you will not harm her. Help her, will you?"

"All right." Ronnie could see his dad getting pale. "Your wish is mine. If you say so, I will."

"Thank you, son. You will be a good leader some day."

"Rest now. You need to rest." Ronnie hugged his dad and quietly slipped away.

Ronnie picked up a handful of fruit and a handful of bread and walked towards the opening that connected his home to Vicky's old home. When Ronnie crawled through the opening, Cookie was sleeping right underneath him.

Cookie opened her eyes slowly. She recognized the mouse from the night she called to him from the rooftop ledge. She had not had food or water for almost two days. Ronnie could see that Cookie was very weak.

Ronnie threw the food down and snarled, "Andy is dead now because of you. I HATE you! As soon as you get well you should leave our house." Ronnie quickly pulled himself back through the opening.

Cookie couldn't believe what she heard. How could Andy be dead? Her tears dripped onto the fruit and bread as she ate. She didn't want to think about her future or how she would survive without Andy. When the food was gone and her stomach was full, Cookie crawled to the space under the vent to lie down. She could feel a light, fresh breeze on her face. Cookie knew she was trapped in the attic. She cried softly, for herself and for Andy, until she fell asleep again.

Chapter Four

Cookie awoke to what she thought sounded like thunder, but she could see that the night sky was clear and bright with stars. The sound came again and suddenly the attic floor began to shake and the chain in the hole was moving and shaking. Cookie quickly crawled to the hole.

Cookie could see dozens of humans wearing all white. One at a time they jumped to kick the bag, which rattled the entire attic floor. It looked dangerous. Cookie couldn't understand why they kept doing that.

Looking carefully, Cookie noticed that all the humans were wearing the same white clothes but some had different-colored pieces of cloth tied around their waists. She saw white, blue, red, and black. The humans with black pieces were stronger and faster than the others.

Cookie couldn't take her eyes off of them. She didn't know what she was watching, but it looked fun and exciting. Sometimes they screamed loudly and that made Cookie's heart jump, but she knew they weren't trying to harm her.

When they stopped kicking the bag, the humans looked like they were fighting, but they never hurt each other. Cookie saw an older man with the black piece clap his hands. When the other humans heard the clapping they stopped fighting. The humans smiled, shook hands with each other, and got in straight lines.

The humans all bowed to the man that clapped his hands. That man was standing in front of them. He looked like the leader. Cookie noticed that his black color was old and faded. The leader talked to the other humans, but Cookie couldn't understand what he was saying. The humans shook hands with the leader and left the building. A few minutes later, when everyone was gone, the leader turned off the light and left the building too.

Cookie looked into the dark room below and sighed. The loneliness came back again. She didn't know what would happen to her tomorrow.

The next morning, the mouse came back again and dropped the food next to the opening. Cookie called, "Who are you? What is your name?"

Ronnie looked at her over his shoulder. "None of your business." Then he left. Cookie decided not to eat.

At lunchtime, Ronnie noticed that Cookie had not

eaten the food he left that morning. "I don't care whether you eat or not. All I'm doing is my job."

Cookie pleaded, "Where is Andy? Is Andy really dead?"

Ronnie didn't say anything and left.

That evening, Ronnie told his father that they should stop wasting their food on the stupid squirrel since she was refusing to eat. Ronnie's father was very ill but decided to visit Cookie.

Ronnie helped his dad through the opening in the wall but refused to go with him. "Are you Cookie?"

Cookie turned to see an older mouse. She instantly knew that this mouse was related to Andy. "Yes, I'm Cookie. Who are you?"

"I am Andy's father."

"Can I ask you a question? Who is the mouse who brings my food?"

Ronnie's dad glanced back at the opening to see Ronnie step out of view. "He is my son and Andy's twin brother, Ronnie."

"Where is Andy?" Cookie braced herself for the worst. In her heart, she knew the answer to her own question.

"Andy is dead."

Cookie's heart sank. "How did Andy die? Was it an enemy cat or another animal?"

"No. It was another mouse; it's a family matter. It's a long story and I don't want to talk about it now." Ronnie's dad coughed heavily. "I want you to eat your food so you can get well. Stay in this attic. The other mouse families will not harm you, but they will not welcome you either. All you need to do is get well as soon as possible and then go to find your family. They must be worried about you. Please eat."

"Thank you, I will." Cookie watched the weak, old mouse crawl back through the opening. "You look ill. Take care of yourself."

"I will." Ronnie's dad coughed again and then disappeared through the opening, where Ronnie's arms were waiting to help his dad.

Ronnie helped his dad climb down from the opening. His dad was getting worse. The physical injuries from the soldiers' attack caused internal damage. His coughs were deep and shaky. His face was so pale. Ronnie helped his dad lie down, then went to feed Cookie.

As his dad tried to sleep Andy's death continued to haunt his dreams. He was getting weaker, as was his desire to live. How could all of this have happened? When Spence allowed his soldiers to beat him yesterday his mind hurt more than the cuts and bruises.

Spence's father died when Spence was young, so Andy's dad had always treated Spence as one of his own blood. Ronnie, Andy, and Spence had been good friends until the situation with Vicky.

When Ronnie wanted to marry Vicky, his dad knew that Andy and Spence also cared for her. Vicky loved only Ronnie. But to keep peace in the family, his father made both of his sons give her up. Ronnie blamed Andy and never seemed to forgive him. He became cold to Andy. And Andy just ignored Ronnie. His dad now regretted stopping the marriage.

When his dad saw him crawling back through the opening, he called to him, "Ronnie, how is she doing?

Ronnie shrugged. "Oh, she is beginning to eat."

"I hope you will not forget Andy's wish."

"I won't."

"I am dying, son. I didn't tell you because I didn't want you to worry."

"Tell me what?"

"When I cough, blood comes with it. I am seriously hurt inside. You must take care of the family now. You are not alone in this world. Take care of your mother and sister." He coughed heavily and continued to ramble, "Son, I always tried to protect our family and provide a safe and comfortable home, but it's so hard. You know, when I was young my father passed away. I blamed a lot on him. Mr. Max took me in and treated me like a son while Spence's father was alive. Spence's father and I were good friends. But after Mr. Max's son died in the terrible accident, Mr. Max became distant. He never said anything, but his eyes told me so. If I had my father, my father could have explained everything and made Mr. Max understand. Son, I am sorry for you. I am dying. You should take care of your mom and sister. You can do it." He coughed again and blood stained his chest. After a few shallow breaths, his breathing faded away.

Ronnie began to shout, "Oh no! Dad! Please don't do this to me."

His mom fell to her knees by his side. She was in

deep grieving but expressed no emotion. There was nothing they could do. Ronnie hugged his sister as she cried.

When Ronnie returned from taking his dad's body to the bushes, he roared, "I'm going to KILL Spence!"

Ronnie's mother shouted, "Hasn't there been enough death? Ronnie, I'm worried about you. You're in charge of this family now. You cannot be so impulsive and vengeful." She grabbed him and hugged him tight.

Ronnie slumped down on the floor, completely exasperated. He asked Sissy to please feed Cookie from now on. He picked up two handfuls of food and placed them into Sissy's arms. He didn't want to talk to or see Cookie. Ronnie wanted to blame Cookie for the loss of his brother and dad, but he knew that some of the blame was his to bear.

Sissy and Cookie became friends instantly, and after Sissy's first visit, Cookie knew their family's history. Sissy told Cookie about everything—the burnt vitamins, Vicky, Spence and his needle weapon, Spence's soldiers, Andy's death, their dad's death, and Ronnie's temper.

By the time Sissy left, Cookie was smart enough to wonder what her role would be. Cookie knew that when she became well again her strength and power would be more than Spence's because she was bigger than any mouse. She thought about killing Spence to avenge Andy's death, but she didn't know how to fight. The needle weapon that Spence carried bothered her, but if she was fast enough, she could protect herself. Instantly

Cookie remembered the humans in the white clothes that were kicking the bag.

Except for Sissy, who came regularly with meals and news about the family, Cookie was usually alone. She decided to spend her time alone learning from the humans.

Cookie thought that if she could learn how to protect herself, she could use what she learned from the humans against Spence or any other enemy that tried to hurt her. As Cookie watched through the chain's hole, hours turned into days. All she did was eat, sleep, and watch the humans train below. She began to understand human language and the martial arts.

Cookie soon learned that the different-colored pieces were called "belts" that the humans earned. Cookie now understood the significance of the colored belts displayed in order on the wall: white, yellow, orange, green, purple, blue, brown, red, red tip, black tip, and black belt. She knew humans with white belts were beginners and those with black belts were more advanced. Beginning with white belt, each belt's color darkened to symbolize the increase in knowledge and ability as the students advanced to Black Belt.

She noticed that different groups of humans with different-colored belts would come and go at different times of the day. She learned that these were called classes. Sometimes she saw small children and sometimes only adults. They were called "students."

The students greeted each other and showed respect to darker belts by bending their bodies in half. They called this "bowing." And every student in every class showed great respect to the leader with the old and faded black belt. They called him Master.

One night during class the Master asked his students to sit down. Cookie listened carefully as the Master spoke.

At the beginning of every class we begin by reciting the Grandmaster's motto, "Thinking before acting," and at the end of each class we end by reciting our School's Values, "Honesty, humility, patience, diligence, and sincerity." These principles and values should not only define our training in the martial arts but should also apply to the commitments in our lives outside our school.

When we study the martial arts, we must truly understand the meaning of the "Do." Many people say the Do is "the way of life," but our Grandmaster believes that the true meaning of Do is "the *right* way of life." In life we must know the difference between right and wrong.

In a way, anything would be possible if there was no right and wrong, but this is a very dangerous attitude for defining and conceptualizing the Do and life. The true meaning of Do should extend into our daily lives. Many ruin or corrupt their lives with their gifts and talents because they don't have strong principles or values.

Simply knowing the meaning of a word does not help our lifestyle, behavior, character, or actions. Now that we understand the true meaning of Do, we should practice it in our martial arts training as well as in daily life. That is why the Grandmaster's vision for his students is for them to be successful in martial arts and in life.

Chapter Five

Ronnie never gave up the thought of revenge. He had spent the past few days collecting toothpicks from Mr. Gyro's restaurant. He knew Spence had a needle weapon, but he couldn't find any needles in any of the shops.

Ronnie knew that Spence had gotten his needle from the fabric store in the new shopping center. That new shopping center was huge. There were so many different stores. Spence and his soldiers could get anything they wanted.

But if Ronnie was going to fight against a needle weapon, he would need a weapon of his own. Even though the tips broke easily, toothpicks were simple to use and already sharp.

Ronnie tried pencils, but they were heavy and hard to hold with one hand. A brand-new pencil was much too large for one mouse to handle. The small, sharp pencil stubs could be used, but they were hard to find now that he needed them. Humans usually threw those pencils away because they were too small to write with. Ronnie had seen the pencil stubs many times before but never thought he would need one as a weapon.

Mice normally fought by hand. They could scratch, bite or hit. But ever since Ronnie saw Spence's cruelty with the needle weapon, it gave him a new direction of fighting. He now believed that as long as you win, anything goes.

Ronnie was recruiting friends from other mice families in the attic to fight. When his friends heard about Spence's brutality, they knew that no mouse was safe. They wanted to defend their families and homes. Ronnie's men knew that sooner or later Spence would make trouble for them or their families.

During her meals with Sissy, Cookie learned that Ronnie was building an army to fight against Spence. Sissy seemed very worried about Ronnie's safety. At that moment, Cookie decided it would not be a good idea to mention her own plans to avenge Andy's death.

Cookie continued to watch every class. She was so excited to learn. Her understanding of the human language improved. She could now figure out most of what she heard. She learned that the white clothes the students wore were uniforms called a "do bok," and the school they had class in was called a "do jang." Cookie also figured out that the clapping meant "stop." When the Master clapped his hands, the students immediately stopped what they were doing to listen.

During a white belt class, Cookie carefully watched as students stood with their feet twice as far apart as their shoulders. The Master stressed the importance of keeping their hips down, knees bent, and toes pointed forward. This was called a Horseback Riding Stance. Cookie imitated the students.

Next the White Belts learned how to make a fist. With both palms opened and facing the ceiling, the students curled the four fingers into the palm. The thumbs were then rested against the index and middle finger. The students pulled both hands back onto their waist. The left hand was extended from the waist while rotating the wrist until the palm was facing the floor. Cookie tried to copy the students but her right arm didn't cooperate with her at all.

Black Belts moved around the room, checking each fist for correctness and reminding students to relax their upper body while keeping their lower body solid. Then each time the Master yelled the students alternated punches right and left with a powerful thrust. Each time a punch was executed the students yelled. When the students finished, the Master explained.

> The tip of your tongue must touch the middle of the roof of your mouth. This will prevent your saliva from entering your lungs and help you breathe smoothly and deeply. This smooth, deep breathing will allow more oxygen to enter your body.

Most of the time, we only use 20% of our lung capacity. But the more you practice deep breathing, the more oxygen your lungs will be able to take in. This will help us burn more calories, promote good health, and increase physical power too.

The tongue is a life form energy switch. When you practice martial arts, you must be aware of your tongue switch. The human body has physical energy and life form energy, sometimes called internal energy.

You are learning the physical part first—kicking and punching—but in the meantime you need to practice your breathing, too. Inhale and exhale smoothly, softly, steadily, silently, and slowly. Practice while you are reading, working, running, fighting, or whatever you are doing. This will help develop your control. Mastery of the martial arts means control of mind and body.

Cookie tried to practice deep breathing. It seemed natural to her. Cookie realized that when her neck and shoulder were injured she had learned to inhale and exhale the correct way to relieve her pain. Her regular breathing had naturally become deep breathing. Now she just had to remember to touch her tongue to the top of her mouth.

Spence wasn't dumb. He had received word from one of his patrol soldiers that a few days earlier Ronnie's dad had died. Andy and his dad were both gone now. Spence knew that Andy's family, especially Ronnie, would seek revenge.

For his own safety, Spence doubled the number of soldiers that walked with him. He would normally go out with only five or six, but now he took more than a dozen. Spence knew that Ronnie's shopping center did not have the potential for more than a dozen fighters. Spence knew his soldiers could beat Ronnie and his men easily, but he didn't want to take any chances. Following Spence's orders, his soldiers paid a visit to the fabric store, and now every soldier carried a needle weapon.

Cookie hadn't heard anything more of Ronnie's army. Sissy thought maybe Ronnie had calmed down. "He was just so angry about Andy and Dad. He wasn't thinking clearly." Cookie could tell that Sissy didn't really believe that Ronnie had calmed down.

Cookie was still excited about her martial arts training. She learned that the students yelled to develop their inner strength and confidence. This yell was called a "ki yap." Cookie knew that yelling in the attic was not a good idea.

She also learned to kick. She could tell that a kick was a lot more powerful than a punch. And because of her right arm, Cookie knew that kicks would be important in defending herself.

She copied the students as they practiced front snap kicks. The students brought their knee up first to aim and then snapped their leg out to contact an imaginary opponent with their foot. Alternating left and right, the students yelled with each kick. Cookie could see that front snap kicks would be useful against a charging opponent.

The Master clapped his hands.

> In life, we will face many obstacles. There is more than one way around an obstacle. A lot of times, people think there is only one way. They stop, give up and become frustrated and angry. We should learn different ways to overcome. That's why the Grandmaster wants you to study the ABC method. This method creates three different variations of the same kick. To begin with they will seem a little difficult, but once you learn them you will be able to use these kicks in a variety of situations. Open your mind, open your eyes, and open your ears to new possibilities. This is mastery of the art.

The students—and Cookie—copied the Master as he demonstrated the ABC front snap kick. Method A was the same waist-level kick they had already practiced. Method B was a lower kick using the big muscles of the leg, and the emphasis was on making the recoil faster than the kick itself. Method C was a higher kick that was stretched to reach out as far as possible, while the upper body, not the head, leaned back for balance.

The Master demonstrated how the ABC kicking variations applied to the side kick, back kick, axe kick, spinning hook kick, and roundhouse kick. He emphasized that the roundhouse kick was the most practical kick to use in fighting because it was excellent for counterattacks. The students paired off and practiced the ABC kicking variations.

The advanced students performed all those kicks on the ground and jumping in the air. That allowed a lot of variety and power. Cookie was amazed at how easy the jump kicks looked. However, the first few times she tried the jump kick, she lost her balance and fell down. Cookie realized that her limp arm was affecting her balance, but she refused to give up.

Ronnie had recruited eleven men. He knew that a surprise ambush was the best plan of attack. So Ronnie and his soldiers hid in the bushes to watch for Spence's patrol. They waited quietly in the bushes, using only hand signals to communicate.

Finally, they heard footsteps approaching. When they saw Spence's patrol pass by, their mouths dropped open. Ronnie and his men couldn't believe their eyes. Each of Spence's soldiers held a sharp needle weapon that glistened in the sunlight.

Ronnie's men dropped their toothpicks and clasped their hands over their mouths. They were imagining the needles piercing their hearts. They knew their toothpicks were useless against the needles. Ronnie could see his men trembling. Spence's patrol passed by, completely unaware of Ronnie's men cowering in the bush.

Ronnie was the only one still holding his toothpick. He began to grit his teeth. Ronnie believed that Spence's soldiers were no different than his men, except that Spence's soldiers had needle weapons. He thought that if his men had those steel needles they would be braver. Ronnie was so discouraged when he returned home from the bush. He knew his men needed motivation and encouragement. But how?

Cookie enjoyed talking with Sissy during meals even though their conversations had become shorter. Now that Sissy was older, she had to learn to gather food for the family. This meant shorter visits with Cookie.

Cookie used her time alone to watch classes and practice. And through painstaking practice, Cookie improved her coordination and finally learned how to maintain her balance during jump kicks.

She also learned that the body could be divided into three sections: high, middle and low. As Cookie practiced her punches and kicks, she aimed for each section's central target. First Cookie kicked her imaginary opponent above the neck in the high section but aimed for the philtrum, which was between the nose and the upper lip. She remembered that striking here would shake the brain and cause a concussion. Then Cookie kicked her imaginary opponent in the chest but aimed for the solar plexus, which is the center of the chest at the weakest point. A blow here would shock the lungs' nerve control and stop breathing. This would knock the wind out of her opponent. Finally, Cookie kicked below the waist in the low section but aimed for the lower abdomen, below the navel, which is a few inches below the belly button. Contact to this area causes the intestines to cramp or, if powerful enough, can lead to severe internal injury.

During a children's class, Cookie heard the Master explain the origin of the three basic stances in martial arts. The Master compared these stances to mountain climbing.

How do we climb up a mountain? We walk. As we climb, our front leg supports most of our body weight, thus bending the front knee, while the rear leg extends straight back for balance and support. We call this Open Stance or Front Stance.

How do we climb down a mountain? The opposite of up is down. So we must now put our body weight in our rear leg, thus bending this rear knee. We call this Back Stance or L Stance.

How do we move horizontally across a mountainside? We keep our body weight even on both legs and bend both knees to provide a stable footing. We call this Horseback Riding Stance.

You are probably wondering how these mountain climbing stances became part of martial arts. Well, we are fortunate that nowadays we practice inside schools like this one. But in the old days people had to practice outside.

Many times students had to climb up or down mountains to find an open area to practice their martial arts. They naturally practiced Open Stance, Back Stance, and Horseback Riding Stance.

So when you practice making a good solid stance, imagine yourself on a mountain.

Ronnie decided that the only way to motivate his men was through his own bravery. He decided that he would sneak into Spence's territory alone. Ronnie could scout out the new shopping center and get an idea of how many soldiers Spence had in his army.

Ronnie searched the shops in his shopping center to find a more suitable weapon. The only weapon he could find was another toothpick, but he also found a steel thumbtack in Mr. Gyro's restaurant. Mr. Gyro had a bulletin board filled with thumbtacks at the front door for customers to add their business cards or advertisements. Ronnie thought the steel thumbtack might block an attack by the needle weapon.

Ronnie held the thumbtack in one hand and the toothpick in his teeth as he crawled out of the telephone cable entrance and down to the parking lot. Ronnie moved quickly from bush to bush. His heart was racing.

It was the perfect night. There was no breeze to carry his scent, and the moon was hiding behind clouds, making it very dark.

As Ronnie got closer to Spence's shopping center, he got down on his knees and began to crawl. His eyes burned with revenge for the deaths of his dad and brother.

He realized now that he should have gotten along better with Andy. Ronnie loved Andy deep down, but as they grew up Andy was recognized as the smarter, more mature twin. So naturally, Ronnie became jealous of his brother. Ronnie always seemed to be second to

Andy, except with Vicky.

Vicky liked Andy as a friend, but she loved Ronnie as a future husband. Andy was not ashamed about his passion for Vicky and continued to pursue her. This caused conflict between Ronnie and Andy. Their dad had no choice but to forbid both of them from pursuing Vicky. Ronnie regretted letting Vicky come between him and his twin brother. His heart ached.

Cookie was really beginning to understand how to fight and defend herself. She learned how to block and dodge attacks.

During an advanced black belt class, Cookie watched students break boards with their hands with little effort. That was amazing to Cookie. However, when she punched the floor it was extremely painful. Cookie now understood why the Black Belts toughened their hands.

She decided that she would begin toughening her knuckles by doing knuckle push-ups. The push-ups were very hard, especially with one arm. Her right arm could only hang lifeless as she pushed with her left. Cookie could only do three, but she decided to keep practicing.

As the students rushed to clean up the broken wood and line up, the Master made his way to the front of the room. He motioned for the students to sit down.

It is important to remember that there are five different versions of power. These Power Principles can be applied to punches, kicks, and blocks.

The first, the focus version, is strong but stops in front of the target to practice perfect control.

Second, the penetrate version is piercing and must pass through the target a few inches. We just used this version to practice our breaking technique.

Third, the recoil version is return. The distance is longer than the focus version and shorter than the penetrate version but the return must be quicker than the extension. This version develops multiple movements.

Fourth, the tension version is heavy. It's like moving under water or moving with heavy weights. It uses slow, concentrated movements.

And finally, the fifth is the natural version. These movements are soft but combine some aspects of all the other versions.

Remember each of these Power Principles as you develop your techniques. Deciding which version to use in which situation will be challenging, but with practice, practice, practice you will understand their benefits.

"Cookie, what are you doing?"

Cookie jumped. She didn't realize that Sissy had been standing behind her.

"Oh, I was just watching the humans." Cookie walked over to sit down next to Sissy.

"What are they doing?"

"Martial arts."

"What is that?"

"It's great! Would you like to try?" Cookie put her

fruit down and got to her feet.

Sissy sighed, "No thanks."

Cookie could tell that Sissy had something else on her mind. "How is your family?"

Tears welled up in Sissy's eyes. "Mom is worse than ever. She is grief stricken." Sissy rubbed her eyes. "Mom is very worried about Ronnie. He has been out all day and no one's seen him. I hope Ronnie is okay. I don't think my mom could handle another death right now. She doesn't talk very much anymore. And since my dad died, I have not seen her smile."

Cookie rubbed Sissy's back. "Do you think Spence would hurt Ronnie?"

"I think so. Spence has been a little crazy ever since his parents died."

"How did his parents die?"

Sissy sniffled, "Both of his parents were killed at the same time by a car. Their deaths hardened Spence. He was always mischievous and conceited, but after his parents died, he became cold, aggressive, and overpowering."

As Cookie listened to Sissy she realized that Spence was all alone like herself. "How did Spence survive alone?"

"His grandfather, Mr. Max, took care of him. Spence was an only child, so Mr. Max spoiled him rotten. At that time, Mr. Max was the most powerful mouse in the new shopping center. Spence took over when Mr. Max passed away."

"*Siss-ssy!*"

Cookie and Sissy looked toward the opening in the wall. They could hear her mom calling for her.

"Ooh! I've got to go. See you tomorrow." Sissy ran to the opening, waved goodbye, and was gone.

Cookie worried about Sissy. They had become best friends. Really, they were like sisters. She wanted to help Sissy but knew there was nothing she could do trapped in the attic. Cookie's worry turned into frustration. She heard the door in the school downstairs close, but then she noticed that a light was still on.

Next to the chain's hole, Cookie sat and looked down to see the Master all alone. Classes were over, but the Master was sitting down in the middle of the room. His legs were crossed, his back was straight, and his hands were touching his stomach.

Cookie jumped when the phone rang but the Master didn't move. This was very strange. His eyes were open so Cookie knew he wasn't asleep. What was he doing? Then Cookie remembered. It must have been a week ago. But she remembered listening to the Master talk about this. It was called Meditation.

She had never seen it before; she had only heard the Master talk about it. She tried hard to remember the class. Cookie recalled that the sitting position was just one of many ways to practice meditation, but one of the most comfortable.

About an hour later, the Master patted his whole body with the palms of his hands, gently stretched his arms and legs, and then turned off the light and left the school. Cookie slid a few inches back from the chain's hole and considered everything she just saw.

Cookie crossed her legs, straightened her back, eyes half closed, and held her right hand on her stomach with her left. After a few minutes, she realized crossing her legs was uncomfortable, but as she concentrated harder on her breathing her focus went to her lower abdomen instead of her legs.

With the tip of her tongue touching the middle of the top of her mouth, she practiced her deep breathing. Cookie emptied her mind and counted her breaths. The more she focused on her breathing, the more she felt like her body didn't exist, including her injured arm.

She could not meditate nearly as long as the Master. Thoughts of Sissy, Andy, Ronnie, the enemy hawk, and her family continued to disrupt her count. Cookie patted her body and stretched like the Master. As she lay down to sleep, she felt calmer than she did after Sissy left. Cookie decided that she would practice meditation every day.

Chapter Six

Ronnie had been waiting in the bushes for hours. When Ronnie had arrived at the entrance of the shopping center, Spence's guards were in large groups on patrol. And each patrol group was relieved by another group of soldiers. The entrance was never left unattended, and the guards watched the area carefully. Ronnie had hoped that at night there might only be one or two soldiers around, but that was not the case. So he watched and waited.

During a shift change, one of the guards finishing duty looked towards the bushes and began walking towards Ronnie. Had he been discovered? Ronnie crouched down lower. The guard stopped directly in front of Ronnie, his foot inches away from Ronnie's nose. The guard moved over to the bushes beside Ronnie.

To Ronnie's relief the guard was just going to the bathroom. Ronnie noticed that the other guards were not watching the bushes. What an opportunity. He had to take it.

Ronnie jumped up, grabbed the guard by the neck, and pulled him into the bushes. The guard didn't have time to scream. As the guard struggled with Ronnie's grip, he dropped his needle. Ronnie didn't hesitate. He picked it up and stabbed the guard in the leg. The guard screamed, "Aaughh!"

The other soldiers on guard began running towards the bushes. Ronnie ran. His legs were moving his feet faster than he had ever run before. After Ronnie climbed into the telephone cable entrance, he realized he was still holding the guard's bloody needle.

By the time breakfast was over, Cookie knew the details of Ronnie's confrontation with Spence's guard. Sissy seemed relieved that her brother was not hurt but worried that Spence might retaliate. But Sissy was happy to report that Ronnie had agreed, due to their mom's pleas, to stay in the attic for the next few days to lay low.

Cookie spent those uneventful days training harder than ever. She could now do fifteen knuckle push-ups and meditate twice as long. Her flexibility had almost doubled, which made her kicks higher and stronger. She also learned how to make a silent ki yap in her lower abdomen.

Cookie felt stronger and healthier than ever. She

learned different variations and uses for kicks, punches, blocks, attacks, grabs, steps, locks, throws, and weapons. And in an advanced black belt class, Cookie learned eight different traditional postures from the Master.

> These postures develop a solid foundation, like a big tree with big roots. The more we practice these postures the stronger our foundation. The practitioner will be like the tree…unmovable.

Cookie admired the Master's wisdom and experience. She hoped that one day she would be a Master. Cookie loved the story the Master told about collecting rocks.

> In the old days, instructors did not take attendance to keep students on track for earning their black belt. Each time a student finished their practice they would pick up one small rock. They put these rocks in a jar. When the jar was full, it was time to move to the next step or belt.

Cookie would dream of training in the mountains just like the Master said. In the dream, she picked up rocks each time she practiced and put them in the attic. The rocks became an enormous pile, almost filling her room. As she placed one more small rock on the pile the floor began to crack. The rocks, and Cookie, fell through the attic floor and into the martial arts school. As she bounced on the mat, she would always wake up giggling. She hoped that someday the dream would come true.

Ronnie spent his time in the attic reassembling his men. He knew that Spence would consider the attack on his soldier an act of war. And his men now understood the seriousness of the situation.

Ever since Ronnie returned with the bloody needle his men seemed more confident. All of them agreed to fight until Spence's army was defeated. Ronnie and his men believed that even if they were killed it was worth their family's survival and honor.

Ronnie knew Spence would come attacking his shopping center. He needed to block the telephone cable entrance at night. Ronnie and his men collected rags from Mr. Gyro's restaurant to block the entrance. Ronnie thought this was a lot easier than having one of his men stand guard. There was no reason to waste manpower before the fighting even started.

Ronnie knew that the only other way Spence could get in was through the secret entrance, which was impossible to block with rags. It was a large hole located in the ceiling. The only other way to protect their families would be to block the opening that connected to Cookie.

Ronnie thought that, in an emergency case like this, his father would understand his decision to block the opening. Anyway, Ronnie believed that even when Cookie got well she would not be able to get out of the attic to find her family. The opening in the wall was too small for Cookie to fit through, and the only other way out was the way she came in. It would be impossible to reach or jump out with one arm.

Ronnie still hated Cookie. The only reason he had not allowed Cookie to starve to death was because he wanted to keep his promise to his father. Ronnie tried to convince himself that now he had no choice. Ronnie would have to sacrifice Cookie's life to save the mice families.

Cookie and Sissy ate quietly. Sissy was very angry as she told Cookie about Ronnie's decision to block the opening. Sissy hugged Cookie. "Be careful. If Spence's soldiers come to attack through the rooftop's secret entrance, they may try to harm you."

After Sissy crawled through the opening, Cookie could see Ronnie's men filling the hole with small rags until the light from the other room was gone. Only the light from the martial arts school lit Cookie's room.

Cookie kneeled down next to the light. The students were sitting in rows and listening to the Master.

As we study the martial arts, we can learn a lot from each other, but also consider the teachings of nature. In our search for the true meaning of life, anyone and anything can be our teacher if we want to learn and improve. For example, water has five virtues.

Number one, water always knows the way to go. If water is spilled, normally it does not just sit there. It flows and continues to move until it reaches its destination. This is *perseverance*. We too must continually move and be persistent in reaching our goals in life.

Number two, water never gives up. When water is flowing, it does not allow obstacles to block its path. Water will push, go around, and go over objects blocking its path to reach its destination. This is *indomitable spirit*. We too must not allow obstacles to keep us from reaching our goals.

Number three, water moves others as it moves itself. Think of a river carrying seeds downstream to flourish in new soil. This is *leadership*. We too should encourage and help others to reach their goals. It's true, it is lonely at the top, so take a few friends with you to keep you company. Be a role model and example for others to follow.

Number four, water never loses its identity. Water can be boiled, frozen, and evaporated, but it is always the same water. This is *sincerity*. We too must stay true to ourselves. Do not change your identity for personal benefit and gain by cheating, faking, lying, or betraying. We must remember who we are, and our values, our morals, our principles.

Number five, water sacrifices itself to clean others. Water washes the dirt and filth from our clothes, our dishes, our bodies. In return it is left polluted. This is *selflessness*. We should be eager to give our time, talent, and wealth to help friends, family, and those less fortunate. This is one of the true spirits of martial arts.

These five virtues define our student oath: "I will

train my mind, body, and spirit to grow in a positive manner; I will practice honesty, discipline, and respect; and I will use what I've learned to help myself and others."

This oath was made for us by our Grandmaster to cultivate our mind and body. He believes that we can improve the understanding of the student oath with our understanding of nature. Consider the teachings of a tree, rock, or mountain. The door is always open for those who seek wisdom.

Cookie realized that if Spence's soldiers did attack through the secret entrance, she would have to defend herself. The only other choice would be to leave, and that was not an option. Cookie could not reach the vent. And even if she could reach it, she did not want to leave. She wanted to help Sissy. Cookie realized that her martial arts training was not only important for her own safety, but for the protection of Andy's family as well.

Early the next morning, Ronnie got reports that Spence's soldiers were spying on his shopping center. Ronnie expected this. He knew Spence would not attack blindly. Ronnie suspected that Spence was sending some of his men to observe his shopping center and report any activity before sending his army.

Ronnie decided to take this opportunity. He would capture Spence's soldiers and hold them prisoner. This would prevent Spence from receiving information and deter Spence from sending any further spies.

Ronnie chose two of his fastest men to go with him. He ordered his men to block the entrance behind them. They made their way down the wall, across the parking lot, and into the bushes near the dumpster. From the bushes, Ronnie could see that the telephone cable entrance was securely blocked. Because of this, he knew Spence's soldiers would never suspect him to be outside.

Ronnie and his men crouched quietly in the bushes and waited. In his hand, Ronnie held the bloody needle he took from the guard. He never cleaned it on purpose. The bloodstains on the needle encouraged his men. It also prevented the reflection of light, which could alert enemies.

When Ronnie and his men heard soft noises coming from over the hill they held their breaths and crouched lower. This time adrenaline pumped in their hearts instead of terror.

Suddenly all sounds stopped. Spence's men were well-trained soldiers. They were trained to move a few steps, lie down, check the area, and then move on. They were very careful and quiet. Ronnie and his men waited. Fighting is not only a competition of strength but of patience.

All of a sudden a small rock landed next to Ronnie's leg. He almost moved but realized it was a trick. He knew it was from one of the soldiers trying to see if anyone was in the bush. After a minute, another rock landed in front of the bush. No one moved.

Ronnie and his men heard the soft noises again. They

lay still. Ronnie spotted two soldiers coming down the hill. The soldiers crossed in front of him, both carrying needles. He nodded to his men to stay down. Ronnie wanted to make sure those two soldiers weren't bait.

No one else was with them.

Ronnie motioned to his men. He would take the biggest soldier and they were to catch the other soldier. In an instant, Ronnie was jumping through the air and onto the back of the biggest soldier.

Ronnie locked an arm around the soldier's neck. The soldier was a lot stronger than Ronnie had anticipated. Ronnie was thrown to the ground. Both of them had dropped their needles. The soldier lunged towards Ronnie. As he wrestled under the soldier, Ronnie could hear his men struggling with the other soldier but didn't have time to see what was going on.

Ronnie managed to reach one of the rocks that the soldiers had thrown earlier. He hit the soldier on the head with the small rock as hard as he could. The solider was knocked unconscious. Ronnie rolled the soldier off of him.

When Ronnie got to his feet, the other soldier was running back over the hill, yelling for help. The soldier had stabbed one of Ronnie's men in the arm and the other in the leg.

Ronnie knew more soldiers would be coming soon. He left the unconscious soldier, grabbed both needles, and rushed his wounded men back to the attic.

At breakfast, Sissy was frantic as she told Cookie about the fight between Ronnie, his men, and Spence's soldiers. Sissy wished for peace, but Cookie knew this incident meant war for certain.

Cookie knew she needed to concentrate on her defense training. She hoped that one of these days she could practice martial arts for enjoyment, not just to survive. If Spence and his soldiers were coming she had to survive or die.

As Cookie practiced her jump kicks with the students, the floor began to rumble and the chain was swaying back and forth. She peeked over the hole to see the Master practicing jump kicks on the bag. Only the Master did not just jump and kick the bag, he jumped and kicked the bag five times before he landed. Cookie's jaw dropped open. It was amazing. Some of the students had even stopped practicing to watch. When the Master became aware of all the curious eyes, he clapped his hands.

> What I'm about to teach you was invented by our Grandmaster. It is called "Um Yang Tae." Translated into English, it means harmony of kick or balancing of kick. In martial arts, there are so many different types of movements. However, all these movements contain one of two elements: linear or circular motions. These two motions can again be divided into half or full movements, creating four possibilities: half-linear, full-linear, half-circle, and full-circle.

The mixture of these possibilities creates hundreds of different types of movements. As martial artists, we cannot practice all these types of movements because of limited time; therefore our Grandmaster has constructed these four possibilities to cover many different movements, and save our time and effort, because eight sets cover these possibilities. A single movement is not as efficient as two movements in one group.

If we practice the mixture of these possibilities, we can have fast, multiple kicks with variety. In a real situation, we can benefit by changing a basic kick into a double kick. And with practice, we will be able to execute multiple kicks in one jump. Our Grandmaster's goal for you is that you can kick a minimum of four times in the air with one jump, which isn't hard, if you practice.

Again, the Master jumped and kicked the bag five times before he landed. Cookie realized her mouth was still open. The theory and numbers were confusing to Cookie, but she tried to copy the movements of the Master. She could only do three so-so kicks. She knew her kicks needed improvement. Kicks were more important for her because of her right arm. She gritted her teeth and continued to practice.

Days went by with no sign of Spence's soldiers. Ronnie was worried. It was too quiet outside, too calm. Ronnie knew Spence's soldiers were not going to spy anymore. The next time he saw them they would come as an army, ready to fight.

Ronnie ordered his men to collect more rags for the entrance and opening. He also prepared a pile of extra rags. Now that Ronnie had attacked his soldiers, he believed that Spence would attack at any time. So Ronnie ordered that the entrance and the opening be blocked all day. This was very inconvenient, but they had no choice.

Ronnie figured that if they had weapons like Spence, they might have a little chance. But there was no way they could get needles. They checked all the shops in their shopping center, including the smelly nail shop, but they could find nothing useful as a weapon. Ronnie's men even tried to take a fork from Mr. Gyro's restaurant, but it was too heavy.

Ronnie would not allow his men to check the martial arts school because he didn't want to see Cookie's face. Ronnie didn't like to think about Cookie. In his mind, Ronnie blamed Cookie for this war. He told his men, "That stupid squirrel has been nothing but a headache since the day Andy found her. All of my family's tragedy started when she arrived. Andy would have never been in Spence's territory that day. Now blood brings blood."

Ronnie was angry but he was comforted by the thought that Cookie was imprisoned in that attic. He let Sissy continue to feed Cookie because he knew the longer she lived the longer she was his prisoner. Ronnie also knew that if Spence did find out about the secret entrance and attacked there, Cookie would surely be killed and justice would be served.

Sissy and Cookie spent almost no time together anymore because the guards hurried her so that they could block the opening. Most of the time Sissy was only allowed to drop off the food and go. Cookie didn't mind. She thought it was safer for Sissy not to be in there just in case Spence attacked.

Cookie practiced Um Yang Tae for hours every day and could now easily make triple jump kicks and 360-degree jump spinning kicks. She could easily do over thirty left knuckled push-ups. And she could now meditate for almost an hour. With all that she had accomplished Cookie was still a little bit nervous because she had never been in a real fighting situation.

It was late, but she wanted to work out one more time. As she bounced and dodged in fighting position, she tried to remember the wisdom of the Master.

> Always prepare to win. If you know yourself and you know your opponent, you can win every time. If you know yourself and you don't know your opponent, you have a fifty-fifty chance of winning. However, if you do not know yourself and you do not know your opponent, you have no chance. Only with luck can you win when you do not know yourself and you do not know your opponent. And in fighting you cannot lean on luck. You must be well prepared.

Cookie began to jog around the room forwards, backwards, and shuffling sideways. Again she tried to focus and concentrate on the words of the Master.

> In fighting, posture is important. How much you leave your body open to an attack makes a difference. Standing diagonally, with your shoulder towards your opponent, protects more of the body from an attack. Also, this diagonal stance allows you to easily shuffle forward and backward in the same stance or walk forward and backward to change stance. These four steps allow you to control your distance from your opponent.

As Cookie lay down to rest, she closed her eyes and practiced her movements in her mind. She knew that one way to increase her power was through mental practice. She thought of the fighting strategy the Master taught.

> In fighting, strategy is important. There are four steps: Search, Advance, Contact, and Control. When you go to the doctor sick, does the doctor give a shot first? No. He looks for symptoms and checks to see what the problem is first.
>
> Search means looking for your opponent's open areas and testing your opponent's reactions. Advance, moving in to take action, occurs only when you understand your opponent and the situation. Contact means execution of the strike, kick, and punch. Finally, Control means managing the situation as well as restraining your own rage or anger.

Cookie jumped to her feet. She could hear Ronnie screaming to his men through the wall. Spence was here!

Chapter Seven

More than two-dozen of Spence's soldiers were at the telephone entrance. They tried ripping and pulling out the rags from the entrance. Each time a rag was taken, Ronnie's men replaced it with one of the extra rags. This went on and on until Ronnie ran out of rags.

When the entrance was almost clear, Ronnie used the needle he had to poke through the rags at the soldiers. After a few stabs into the rags, Ronnie heard one of the guards scream, "Aaarrgh! My arm!"

Now Spence was angry. He ordered his men to use their needles to stab back at Ronnie and his men. Ronnie expected this and moved his men away. He watched as the needles came back and forth. Taking a chance, Ronnie timed it just right and snatched a needle from a soldier's hands.

Now Ronnie had another needle. Spence was livid.

Spence called to the soldier that lost his weapon. As soon as the soldier stood before him, Spence kicked the soldier in the shin, "You stupid idiot! You let him take your weapon?"

Ronnie and two of his men began stabbing their needles through the entrance rags. Spence called to his soldiers, "Let's regroup and attack another time. We'll be back." Spence was embarrassed and frustrated.

Ronnie's men cheered as Spence's soldiers climbed down to retreat. However, Ronnie was even more worried. He knew that next time Spence would not stop until they were all dead. Spence was very ambitious and greedy. And Ronnie had a feeling that Spence was interested in this shopping center for his expansion.

Ronnie knew Spence was coming again soon. Luckily Spence had not discovered the secret entrance. But how long would Ronnie's luck last? If Spence's soldiers came through the rooftop vent, Ronnie could block the opening to Cookie's room. But how long could he leave it like that?

Ronnie knew that, after Spence's soldiers killed Cookie, they could camp out in Cookie's room and outside the shopping center and attack again, and again, and again until all of Ronnie's family and friends were dead. How ironic. Ronnie realized if he closed the opening against Spence's attack, in a way, he would be imprisoning all of them in the attic, like Cookie. They would not have the freedom to go outside, taste fresh air, or run through the bushes.

Ronnie left his men celebrating to collect more rags. His men couldn't comprehend the seriousness of the situation. Ronnie wanted to disappear from this mess.

Cookie could now hear the men laughing and talking. The soldiers were gone. She breathed a sigh of relief. Sissy would not be back until tomorrow for breakfast. She would have to wait until then to hear what happened. Cookie lay down on her back. Her heart was still racing from the excitement.

She placed her hands on her stomach. Cookie had learned to calm herself by practicing reverse abdominal breathing. She not only used it to relax, but also to increase her strength and power with all of the different kinds of defense and attack techniques. Cookie closed her eyes and considered the Master's warning.

> There are two different kinds of lower abdominal breathing: regular and reverse. While both types provide enormous benefits, reverse abdominal breathing will increase a practitioner's strength and power.
>
> Reverse abdominal breathing occurs when you inhale by squeezing the lower abdomen and exhaling by filling the lower abdomen. As you inhale, you must hold your breath in your lower abdomen for as long as you can.
>
> Unfortunately, in their rush to achieve faster results, a lot of practitioners overdo it. This is very dangerous. Without the correct guidance, a

practitioner could suffer serious physical and mental damage, including death. The Grandmaster always warns me about practicing this advanced method.

Without the proper foundations of regular lower abdominal breathing, reverse abdominal breathing is impossible. Some people are born with the natural ability to perform reverse breathing, but this is very rare. Don't count on this being your case.

If you experience any strange symptoms such as dizziness, headache, or increased heart rate, stop immediately and return to normal breathing. When you practice this special breathing use your common sense.

Cookie had been using regular lower abdominal breathing ever since she got injured, so when she first began using reverse abdominal breathing it felt very natural, including holding her breath.

When Spence and his soldiers returned to their shopping center after retreating, Spence was very angry. One of his best soldiers was injured, another lost his weapon, and his strategy had not worked. Spence almost shouted to kill the idiot soldier that lost his weapon, but he knew the other soldiers would be upset so he held his tongue.

Spence turned to his men as they reached the entrance. "Our enemy is a lot smarter than we thought. I would like two-dozen soldiers to volunteer to return to that shopping center in three days and destroy our enemies. In two days, two of our good friends have been attacked and wounded. If we don't straighten this matter out now, then when will we? If you feel that now is the time, who volunteers? Raise your hands!"

Everyone yelled, "NOW is the time!" Every soldier raised his hand.

As he turned and walked into his shopping center, Spence sneered with confidence. He knew everybody would raise their hand. He was glad he held his tongue.

Spence spotted his wife. "I will bring good news in three days." He rubbed Vicky's stomach. "How is my baby doing? When my baby is born, he will have a new playground. I will expand into that old shopping center."

Spence tried to read Vicky's facial expression. Vicky's eyes darted from Spence to the floor. She knew Spence was still jealous of Ronnie, and that the jealousy would never end. Vicky and Ronnie's love was in the past and Spence knew that. Why did Spence continue to punish himself and her?

Love is not a criminal thing for young hearts. It is exciting and thrilling. When time had passed, it becomes a beautiful memory, no more, no less. Vicky tried to erase Ronnie from her memory as much as she could for Spence.

Vicky was still upset about Andy's death by Spence. She felt responsible for his death. Vicky didn't know how she should react. Vicky knew Spence was going to kill Ronnie next. She hated to think about that. Time would solve everything, but Spence tried to get rid of life. Killing Ronnie would not erase his memory or her love for him. Vicky knew she needed time.

At breakfast, Sissy told Cookie everything. Ronnie's men were in such a good mood that they let Sissy visit with Cookie longer so they could hear their story of victory told again. When Sissy told the part about the retreat, Cookie could hear Ronnie's men laughing and cheering in the other room. And when Sissy said goodbye through the opening, Ronnie's men chuckled and patted her on the back for doing such a good job at retelling the story.

Cookie glanced at the vent. Like Ronnie, she knew this was nothing to cheer about. If Spence was everything she had heard he was, he would come again. Cookie shook her head and tried to clear her mind of it all. She tried to remember what she was thinking about before Sissy came for breakfast. "Ah, yes, the five elements."

Cookie was still confused about the five elements: fire, water, wood, metal, and earth. She remembered the Master's lesson on "Um Yang."

> Martial arts were developed several thousand years ago with strong influences from eastern philosophy and culture, and vice versa. At the same time, martial arts and medicine influenced each other. Martial arts soon meant learning self-defense as well as learning how to develop a healthy body and mind. These influences of philosophy, culture, and

medicine on the martial arts defined the "Um Yang" principle.

Um Yang means positive and negative. Um Yang expresses the dualism of the cosmos: positive-negative, day-night, men-women, hot-cold, block-attack, and so on. At the same time, when we study meditation we try to create a healthy balance where below the waist is hot and above the waist is cool. As the martial arts developed, more people began to relate the Um Yang principles with nature's five elements: fire, water, wood, metal, earth.

Again, consider the teachings of nature. Each of the five elements can give life or take life, Um Yang. For instance, water extinguishes fire. Then the water is soaked up by the earth to give life to wood in the form of trees and plants. The earth is then depleted of nutrients by the wood. The wood can then be destroyed by metal tools like an axe and fed to build a new fire.

The relationship of these five elements can also be represented in the human organs: heart-fire, kidney-water, liver-wood, lungs-metal, and spleen-earth. For instance, when people get angry their heart rate increases, their face becomes red, and we have all heard the expression that "our blood begins to boil."

When Vicky's father heard that Spence had to retreat, he decided to give a tip to his son-in-law. He knew this feud had to be settled. Besides, his daughter Vicky was pregnant with Spence's baby, and he wanted his grandchild to have an easy life.

Vicky's father called to Spence. "Spence, if you go to the rooftop on Ronnie's shopping center there is a secret entrance into the attic. There are several vents on the roof, but the old, rusty vent is the one. However, I must warn you, if you go into the vent the only way out is the main entrance, because that vent is located on the ceiling and is impossible to exit. I have thought about it, and there is only one way you can get back out. You must put some kind of rope or stick down in the hole."

Spence shouted, "Why did you wait to tell me that now? Is your heart still over there?"

"No, Spence, you know better than that. I told you there was no way out. If they block the opening connecting the other attics, you will be stuck, starve, and die. If you are lucky enough, you can get down into the martial arts school, but there is no food and no place to hide."

"Well, I'm sorry for shouting. I was angry at myself about this difficult situation." Spence thought a moment and said, "We can carry a big stick and put it in the vent."

"Spence, I think a rope would be easier to carry. You can tie it from outside and lower it to the attic floor."

"Hmm. Good idea. How long should the rope be?"

While motioning with his hands, Vicky's father considered. "Probably around ten times our height to be safe."

"All right. Thank you. No hard feelings."

That day, Spence ordered his soldiers to get two

lenghts of yarn from the fabric store in their shopping center. He thought one line was not enough for a fast attack.

During lunch and dinner, as Sissy came and went, Cookie could still hear Ronnie's men retelling the story of Spence's retreat, especially the part when Ronnie snatched the soldier's needle through the rags. After dinner, when the rags finally smothered the sounds of cheer and laughter, Cookie felt a silent calm.

Cookie crossed her legs easily and put both hands on her stomach. To do this, she had to lay her right hand on her stomach with her left. Cookie followed the Master's instruction and began reverse lower abdominal breathing.

She felt energy circulating from her "bac hae," which is the path from the center of the head to the lungs. The energy moved from her lungs to her lower abdomen, and from her lower abdomen to the "hae yum," which is between the groin and the anus.

Cookie admired the knowledge and ability of the Master. And though the Master often mentioned his Grandmaster to his students, Cookie had not yet seen him.

Cookie tried to refocus. When she practiced meditation, she tried to focus on breathing, but a lot of times she was interrupted by her own thoughts and memories—her parents, the enemy hawk, Andy, Ronnie, Sissy, the Master, the Grandmaster, martial arts training, Spence, and her unknown future—all of these thoughts became thieves that stole her mind.

She tried to lock her mind from these interruptions, but the thief was already inside. Cookie realized that the more she tried to block out the thoughts the stronger they became. She opened her mind instead of closing it. She opened the door and let the thief come in, but she tried to continue focusing on her breathing. She didn't want to lose direction.

The more she practiced her breathing the more her physical strength improved, and mentally she began to taste inner peace. Anything could happen and everything was possible. She could accept that.

Chapter Eight

The next day Ronnie sat alone as he watched his men continue to celebrate. Ronnie knew war was coming. He thought about moving everyone, all of his family and friends, to another place, but there were too many of them, and where would they all go? They had lived in this shopping center for many generations.

He knew that Spence hated him. Ronnie made up his mind. He knew that he would have to leave the shopping center or risk the lives of all his family and friends.

Ronnie thought that if he left the shopping center with Spence's agreement, Spence would spare the lives of his family and friends. Ronnie knew that if he tried to deliver this message to Spence himself, they would kill him on sight and still attack the shopping center. He also knew that if he agreed to leave the shopping center, he would not be able to survive on his own.

Ronnie decided to send a messenger to Spence. He called to his men, "Everybody, I have an idea!" His friends and family gathered around. Ronnie explained his plan.

No one asked any questions. They knew this meant Ronnie was sacrificing his life for theirs. This also meant they would have to surrender to Spence's control. They were very confused and discouraged.

Ronnie knew if there was a delay and Spence moved his men into action, it would be too late. "I need a volunteer to take this message to Spence."

Nobody said anything. Ronnie expected this.

Sissy looked around. Everyone seemed to be more terrified for his or her own safety than concerned for Ronnie's sacrifice.

Ronnie was upset. "I thought you were strong and brave. What's the matter? I know that Spence might try to kill the messenger, but we have to try this first." Ronnie looked out and then pointed. "How about you, John? You are very fast."

"Well ah, y-you know. Um, ah. I'm not a g-good talker," John stuttered.

Ronnie pointed again. "Then Charlie, how about you?"

"Ronnie, I don't mind going, but if I get killed who will take care of my mother?" Charlie shrugged.

Sissy noticed that Charlie was trembling. Everyone else looked at the floor to avoid eye contact with Ronnie.

Sissy shouted, "I WILL GO!"

Later, when Sissy brought fruit and bread to Cookie, Cookie couldn't believe what happened at the meeting. "Sissy, what do you mean? Where are you going? Why are you leaving?"

"Cookie, I may not see you anymore." Sissy's eyes sparkled with tears as she spoke. "I have to go see Spence tomorrow morning." Sissy explained Ronnie's plan.

Cookie was frustrated that there was nothing she could do to help Sissy in this matter. Sissy had always been kind to her. She admired Sissy for being so brave.

Sissy hugged Cookie. "I will ask my mother to take care of you. She will help you. Good luck, Cookie."

As Sissy climbed through the opening and waved goodbye, Cookie's heart ached and tears filled her eyes. Cookie felt alone again. She thought of the enemy hawk, and her loneliness turned into rage.

Cookie hated that enemy hawk. Without that incident, Cookie's family would be living together happily, Andy would still be alive, and Sissy would not be going to see Spence. Cookie remembered her family's tall tree, the sounds of the forest, and all those beautiful creatures. She knew her family was living happily without her. She just hoped that maybe they would think about her every once in a while.

Cookie began practicing her Um Yang Tae. She found that her martial arts training soothed her mind and relieved stress.

She began to fight with one imaginary opponent. Cookie jumped and kicked the imaginary opponent four times before she landed. It was easy. This time she had two opponents…a jumping split kick. No problem. Then she fought three. Spinning back kick, a double roundhouse, and an axe kick. They weren't too hard to handle.

Four, five, six imaginary opponents. She could move near the wall so she could see all of them. Cookie knew she would have to use her kicks as her weapon.

Seven, eight imaginary opponents. She imagined that they now surrounded her from all directions. Cookie started laughing. She had almost forgotten about her tail. Her tail had more strength than both her legs combined and could cover 360 degrees with one spin. Her tail could sweep and push opponents away while she prepared for the next attack.

Nine, ten, eleven imaginary opponents. Cookie practiced long into the night.

Sissy, Ronnie, and their mom got up early the next morning.

"Daughter, I am very proud of you. Our family's blood is courageous. Take care of yourself. I love you." Sissy's mom swallowed her tears.

"Mom, don't worry, I'll be fine. I will. Oh, by the way, can you take care of Cookie while I'm gone? She usually eats triple our portion." Sissy giggled. "Will you promise to take care of her, Mom?"

"Yes, of course."

"Sister, you are a lot braver than any of us." Ronnie hugged Sissy. "I know that you could be a better leader than me. Between you and me, in this shopping center there is no one else that could be a leader. If you want to, I will go to Spence and you stay here. Can you be a leader for our family and friends?"

"No. They need you. Ronnie, remember you are the leader of these families. I cannot organize everything like you. Besides, he will kill you before you can deliver the message of surrender, and then Spence will kick us out or destroy us."

"Sissy, please be careful. Take care of yourself." Ronnie handed Sissy a needle. "Take this with you just in case."

Ronnie hugged Sissy again. He wasn't expecting Sissy to come back. He was so depressed. Even with the fighting between him and Andy, Sissy never took sides and had always been nice to them equally.

"I just want to say goodbye to Cookie before I leave." Sissy hurried to the opening.

Ronnie watched Sissy. She was young, cute and loving. Tears began to run down his face until he couldn't see through the mist of tears. And when he noticed his mom weeping too, he knew she was in pain. She had already lost her husband and son, and now, her daughter. Ronnie felt sympathy for his mother.

Cookie was just beginning her morning stretch as Sissy rushed in.

"Cookie! Cookie, I brought you a weapon." Sissy handed the needle to Cookie.

Cookie was excited to hold the needle. She knew how to use the needle, because she watched as the

Master taught his students how to use a staff.

Without thinking, Cookie began to spin, block, and attack with the needle.

Sissy's mouth fell open. She couldn't believe her eyes. "What are you doing?"

"Martial arts practice with a staff."

"How do you know how to do that?"

"I learned from the Master."

"What?"

"The martial arts Master downstairs." Cookie pointed to the hole with the chain hanging through it. "I learned their language too. But I'm not at the Master level yet. Someday I'd like to become a Master."

"Wow! Cookie, I feel much better about leaving when I know you can protect yourself if Spence attacks."

Suddenly, Cookie stopped spinning the needle. She remembered that Sissy was leaving to see Spence. "Sissy, you keep the needle. I don't need this weapon. I can handle myself. You need it." Cookie handed the needle back to Sissy. "But before you go can I show you a couple of things?"

"Sure!"

Cookie explained, "In an emergency situation always think minimum effort with maximum results. The Master emphasizes vital points. When someone jumps to bite us, we usually turn to run. That really gives them a chance to bite us. So instead try to hit their nose with your palm." Cookie began to demonstrate. "Do not be scared of their open mouth and do not punch inside the mouth. Let's practice a few times."

Sissy practiced on Cookie.

"One more thing, if they try to choke you with their hands, kick them in the groin."

Sissy practiced again. "Thank you, Cookie. You are great. I love you. No wonder Andy loved you so much. I am sure Andy would be very proud of you. I feel much better. Goodbye, Cookie."

"Sissy, you will be okay." Cookie patted her shoulder with her left hand.

They both knew they would never see each other again.

Cookie waited to cry until Sissy left. She wanted to be brave in front of Sissy. Sissy had been like a sister to her, and she was always worried about her safety. As she wiped the tears away, Cookie gasped.

Sissy had left the needle under the opening.

Sissy rushed across the parking lot and into the bushes. She didn't want to give herself time to think about how scared she was. Just as Sissy reached the top of the hill past the bushes, Spence's soldiers were waiting. Three needles glistened as they pointed at her chest.

Sissy slowly raised her arms in surrender. "I don't have a weapon. I came to give Spence a message from Ronnie."

The soldiers nodded to one another and one said, "Let's go."

Sissy was led directly to Spence. She swallowed her

fears long enough to deliver Ronnie's message.

Spence listened and laughed. "Were you the bravest among Ronnie's people? Are all the men dead? Ha, ha. Well, since you are a little girl I will spare your life." Spence waved to his soldiers. "Take our new prisoner away."

That evening, Spence laughed to his wife. "Vicky, guess what? Those chickens sent Sissy to give me a message that Ronnie wants to give up under the condition that I spare his family and friends. It isn't a bad offer. But I don't want to see a second or third Ronnie born."

Vicky was startled. "What do you mean, Sissy? She is a small girl."

"You're right. They sent a little girl. All the men were too scared to come here. The game is over. If they hadn't started this, I would have left them alone."

Vicky knew Spence was making excuses for himself. Ever since she married him, she had never heard him admit a mistake or apologize. He was always right and always perfect. Spence was greedy and ambitious but thought of himself as a visionary. He was driven by the purpose to become a good ruler. Vicky was beginning to realize that Spence had a cruel character.

Vicky looked down at her feet. "What are you going to do with Sissy?"

"Oh, I'm keeping her prisoner."

"Are you not going to let her go home?"

"Why? Do you want me to?"

Vicky tried to act impartial. "It doesn't matter to me."

"Good. I hope you are not emotionally attached to that family. Tonight I will be busy taking care of this Ronnie problem." Spence kissed Vicky. "I'll see you in the morning."

Spence gathered two dozen of his finest soldiers.

"Tonight is the night. We have waited and prepared. Now is the time. When you fight, if you are scared of your opponent you will get hurt or die. But if you want to win, you can win. As you know, there are a lot more of us than them. They already want to surrender. But I refuse to accept their surrender. As your leader, I must not compromise your dignity. Without you, I would not need to be here. Your pride and future are my responsibilities. We will show Ronnie and his men no mercy. Follow me!"

Spence's men erupted, "Let's GOOOOOO!!"

Cookie practiced techniques tirelessly with the needle. Unfortunately Cookie could not use two hands, but she tried to imitate the Black Belts and the Master as much as she could with one hand. She knew the needle could cover more distance and area than her arms and legs.

The needle was light and small for her, but she could use it to understand and learn the principles. She realized angle was an important fact. She had to use more than the eight basic directions of front (north), back (south), left (west), right (east), and the diagonals in between because the longer distance created a larger gap. Cookie now used sixteen directions to cover her open area, like the Master.

The needle became a part of her arm. She was sweating, but she was full of energy. The Master had always emphasized three different ways to attack in staff fighting: hitting, poking, and edge strike. Cookie knew that in defense, rolling, circling, and smacking were the most important and practical techniques.

Cookie thought about the Master's wisdom.

> When you are against an opponent, you must remember there are three different degrees of fighting. If you want to take your opponent's life you must expect to invest your bone. If you want to break your opponent's bone you must expect to invest your skin. If you want to cut your opponent's skin you must know yourself as well as your opponent. That's why fighting is not easy, especially when you try to destroy your opponent without a reason. If you want to be a good fighter you have to believe in yourself first. If you're not sure, run away and do not take a chance.

Cookie thought about all her training and practice. How would she ever know if she was a good fighter? Was she ready to take a chance?

Suddenly Cookie heard footsteps above her head on the rooftop.

Spence had two groups of soldiers. One group was to attack the main entrance, and the other was going to the rooftop. Spence's strategy was to attack through the secret entrance and force Ronnie's men through the main entrance, where Spence's men would be waiting. All of Spence's soldiers clutched shiny needles. His soldiers were excited and full of energy.

Ronnie's men were also divided into two groups. One group guarded the main entrance, and the other was stationed at the opening leading to Cookie's room. Ronnie stayed at the main entrance.

When Ronnie heard movement on the rooftop and voices outside the entrance, he peeked through the rags to see Spence's soldiers waiting. Ronnie taunted the soldiers by shaking the needle at them. "Hey, you chickens, come get your needle. Did anyone lose this?" Ronnie and his men laughed.

The soldiers ignored Ronnie and followed Spence's orders to wait.

Ronnie continued to tease the soldiers. "Hey, where is Spence? Go get him. Tell him I will fight him one on one." Ronnie continued to try and aggravate the soldiers by jabbing at them with the needle.

One of the soldiers became impatient and tried to grab Ronnie's needle. The needle stabbed the soldier in the hand. When the soldiers saw that their friend had been stabbed, they began stabbing into the rags in the main entrance.

Ronnie and his men jumped back from the entrance. Spence's soldiers stepped away from the hole to wait again.

On the rooftop, Spence's soldiers carried yarn to the secret entrance vent. Vicky's father was walking behind Spence, guiding the soldiers to the secret entrance.

As Spence sneered, the moonlight reflected off his teeth and his weapon. He ordered his men to tie the ends of the yarn to the vent and lower it into the hole.

Spence called to his father-in-law, "You know the way. Why don't you go first? We will follow you."

The old man hesitated.

Spence asked, "What's wrong? Are you having second thoughts about your loyalties?"

Spence's father-in-law put down his needle beside the vent and grabbed on to the yarn, his hands trembling. He knew that this would mean the end of Ronnie's family. It didn't seem that long ago that he thought Ronnie would be his son-in-law. Now he was the one leading Spence to kill Ronnie and all his family and friends. He regretted being involved, but it was too late. When Spence asked to marry Vicky and offered them a new house, he permitted Spence to marry Vicky. He never imagined that it would all come to this. Vicky's father tried to hold his tears as he realized Spence had his eye on him.

"Wait a minute. Don't forget your weapon." Spence handed his father-in-law his needle again. "We came here to fight, remember?"

As Vicky's father climbed down, Spence looked at his men. "Let's go one by one on each line."

Cookie backed into a dark corner as she watched the two pieces of yarn come down from the rooftop vent. She knew it must be Spence's army. Her heart was beating in her throat.

Cookie's hands and feet were sweating. All her martial arts training and practice would now be put to the test. She had to survive. She felt more confident when she felt the needle in her hand. The needle made Cookie remember Sissy. Thinking of Sissy gave her courage.

Cookie decided to stay in the shadows and wait. One of the pieces of yarn began to shake. They were coming.

Vicky couldn't sleep. Vicky was very depressed.

When Vicky lived in Ronnie's old shopping center, Sissy was like a baby sister to her. Vicky would always defend Sissy and fuss at Ronnie and Andy when they teased her. Now Sissy was a prisoner in her home. She felt responsible for Sissy's life.

Vicky gathered some bread in her arms and went to the room where Sissy was being held.

The guard stood up to greet her.

"Excuse me." Vicky tried to pass the guard. He stepped in her way.

Vicky could see that Sissy sat in a small room. Her hands and feet were bound. The guard seemed to be watching her carefully to make sure she did not try to chew through her ropes.

The guard apologized. "Sorry, Mrs. Spence, I am not allowed to permit visitors."

"Please. I just want to speak with her. As you know, she was my neighbor."

"I understand, but Spence told me to allow no one into this room."

Vicky realized that nice conversation was not going to get her in to see Sissy. She exaggerated her anger. "You are not going to LISTEN to me!? I'm Mrs. Spence." She smacked the soldier in the face. "Where is your respect?"

The shocked soldier held his cheek. "I'm sorry. She's my responsibility, please understand, Mrs. Spence. Would you keep this visit a secret?"

"Of course I will keep it secret." Vicky forced a nervous smile. "I just want to give her some food. I'm sorry for my temper."

She gently touched the soldier on the arm and slid past him into the room.

"Sissy, you look terrible. I'm sorry for what happened to you, to Andy, and to your family. There was nothing I could do." Vicky held Sissy's tightly bound hands.

"Vicky, I know you tried. I don't blame you. Even after you got married and went away, I still thought of you as my friend."

"Sissy, don't be scared. I will do my best to save your life. You are like a baby sister to me." Vicky hugged Sissy and began to cry.

Sissy tried to wipe Vicky's cheeks, but her hands were useless.

Vicky pulled at the ropes. "What a ruthless thing to tie your hands and feet like this. I wish Spence were here so I could ask him to untie you. As soon as Spence comes back, you will be free. I promise. I will save you, so you don't need to try to escape nor do anything dumb. Spence was upset, but he will be all right."

Vicky spoke very loud on purpose so the guard could hear. She knew the guard was listening to every single word.

"Guard, don't treat her as a prisoner. Can you loosen her hands and feet? It's too tight. She is like my sister. As soon as Spence comes back, I will let her free." Vicky turned to leave. "I will be back from time to time to check on her."

From the shadows, Cookie saw one shaking old mouse come down the yarn. When he reached the floor, he squinted to see around in the dark. Then he shouted to the roof, "Everything looks fine!"

Cookie saw the needle in the old mouse's hand and realized that it was Spence's army. The war had begun.

Without thought, Cookie ran up behind the old mouse and hit his head with a palm strike that knocked the mouse to the ground hard. Cookie stepped next to the mouse and could see that he was not moving or breathing. When Cookie realized the mouse was dead, she decided to restrain and control her power to injure, not kill. The Master always said,

> Martial arts are not for killing. The purpose of martial arts is not the destruction of your opponent; it is to defend yourself and others.

Cookie saw both pieces of yarn shake again. She backed into the dark corner again to wait. After a few seconds, Cookie saw another soldier coming down the yarn. Before he could reach the floor, Cookie's jumping sidekick knocked the soldier into the wall, leaving the soldier with broken ribs and gasping for breath.

Another soldier had already reached the floor when Cookie turned around. Cookie stood like a giant monster in the darkness. The soldier dropped his needle and fainted. Both pieces of yarn began to shake again…more soldiers were coming.

Cookie did not back into the shadows this time. She waited. Two soldiers landed, then two more behind them. Four soldiers were ready with needles to attack. They surrounded Cookie. Cookie grinned while the soldiers shook. Within a split second, Cookie was in the air. A spinning back kick knocked one soldier into his partner and sent them both flying. Cookie quickly turned behind her, grabbed the third soldier's needle and threw the soldier over her shoulder. Cookie's roundhouse kick left the last soldier in the corner with a broken arm.

As Spence climbed down behind two of his men, he stopped at the middle of the line and his jaw dropped open. He couldn't believe what he saw. His soldiers scattered around the room moaning in pain, his father-in-law-dead, and a huge squirrel tossing his men like leaves.

Before Spence could even analyze the situation, Cookie swung her tail and knocked his two soldiers down off the yarn. One of the soldiers tried to stab the squirrel, but she snatched the needle and kicked the soldier in the stomach. The other soldier tried to run back to the yarn, but Cookie's tail caught his leg and threw him into the wall, knocking him unconscious.

Spence was angry. He quickly climbed back up the yarn and out of the vent. He ordered one of his soldiers to bring the soldiers guarding the main entrance. Spence believed they could handle the squirrel if they all attacked at the same time.

As his men gathered around, Spence cleared his throat. "As you know, fighting depends on strength. We have strength in our numbers. There are fifteen of us who are willing to win. There is only one squirrel. All he needs is one stab. Can we do it? Yes, we can do it. We are here to win. Let's go all together and fight until that squirrel is dead! Then victory will be ours!"

Spence's men begin climbing down the yarn two by two.

Vicky visited Sissy again later that night. It was a long night for all of them.

The guard was watching Sissy so closely he had not blinked.

Sissy looked weak and tired.

Vicky knew there was not much time left before Spence would return. Vicky gently touched the guard on the arm. "Hello again, I'm glad to see you are doing your job properly. You are not sleepy?"

"No, ma'am."

"Excellent. I'm glad Spence has someone like you. Loyal. When he comes back I will tell him about you."

"Thank you, ma'am."

"Can I talk with Sissy again? She is so young. I have some more bread for her."

"Yes, ma'am. Sure."

"When Spence gets back, I will make sure she is free. You know that, right?"

"Yes, ma'am."

Vicky moved slowly past the guard. "Sissy, how are you doing? Are you okay? I brought another snack for you." Vicky winked at Sissy.

Sissy was confused. "Thank you. I will eat it later if you don't mind."

Vicky winked again, then grabbed her stomach and screamed. "Aargh! Guard! Guard! Help me. My stomach is beginning to hurt."

The guard hesitated and looked around.

Vicky grasped her stomach and fell to her knees. "Help me, please."

The guard rushed in. With his needle in one hand, he pulled Vicky back up on her feet with the other hand.

As they left the room, Vicky fell to the ground with a scream. "Oh, I think I broke my knee. How can you hold me like that? I cannot move it. There's so much pain in my knee. Go get help. You cannot help me alone."

The guard ran to look for help, yelling, "Can anybody hear me? Mrs. Spence is hurt!"

The guard's voice and footsteps were fading as he

ran farther away. As soon as his voice faded away, Vicky got to her feet and ran back into Sissy's room. She opened the bread and pulled out the piece of broken glass. She used it like a knife and cut Sissy's rope. "Let's go, Sissy. I will show you the way out. Follow me."

When Ronnie and his men heard the soldiers being called from the main entrance to the rooftop, he ran to the opening to Cookie's room. There was a lot of noise coming from Cookie's room.

Ronnie thought, *Why is it taking them so long to attack us?* He knew once they killed Cookie they were coming for the rest of them. Ronnie tried to look through a crack in the cement wall but could not see clearly.

Ronnie wanted to call to Cookie through the crack to ask if she was okay, but he couldn't because of his pride. Waiting was all he could do.

Cookie looked around at the injured soldiers scattered around her room. She shook her head. It shouldn't have happened this way. She hated Spence for killing Andy, but not his soldiers. Without reason, they tried to kill her. She did not understand. She understood the enemy hawk tried to kill her for food. But Spence's soldiers wanted to kill her for no reason except to dominate this shopping center. Cookie felt sorry for Spence's soldiers.

Both pieces of yarn began to shake again. Cookie didn't wait for the soldiers to land. When the soldiers were in sight, she jumped to meet them. Cookie punched one and side-kicked the other at the same time, sending them flying through the air.

Another two soldiers slid quickly down the yarn. As soon as they landed, Cookie roundhouse-kicked one in the face and the other in the stomach.

The soldiers were coming much faster. As the next two soldiers climbed down, Cookie's jumping split kick knocked both soldiers to the ground with a thud.

Cookie only had time to jump and punch one last soldier in the jaw. She landed and turned around to see eight soldiers encircling her from all directions, each pointing his needle at her.

Cookie shouted, "Which one of you is Spence? Step forward!"

In anger, Spence shouted, "I am Spence. Who are you?"

"I am Cookie, a friend of Andy. Are you the one who killed Andy?"

"Yes. It was nothing personal. Andy trespassed on our property. He was trying to steal my wife." Spence looked around the room. "You have hurt a lot of my soldiers. Now you must die. KILL IT!"

When Vicky and Sissy finally snuck out of the shopping center, Vicky hugged Sissy. "My baby sister, be safe. Now you can go back home. Don't worry about me. I can take care of Spence."

Sissy was crying. "As long as I live, I'll never forget what you have done for me. Bye, Vicky."

Sissy turned and ran into the bushes.

She tried to run as fast as she could, but her feet were still sore from the ropes. Sissy could see the hill. She knew that over the hill was her shopping center.

Suddenly, a large mouse grabbed her arm, and a deep voice came from the bush, "You think you can escape. That's too bad. Mr. Spence ordered me to kill you if you tried to escape." He pointed his needle at Sissy's stomach. "Mr. Spence knew you would try to escape. So he ordered me to watch you and the guard. I saw everything that happened in the jail. Mrs. Spence tricked the guard. I have been watching you ever since you were captured. Mr. Spence is very smart. I respect him."

Sissy didn't have a choice. She didn't mind dying, but if this guard lived, Vicky would be harmed. Sissy grabbed the needle with all her might. She hit his nose with her head and kicked him in the groin. As the guard dropped to his knees, she had time to run away. But she had to kill him to protect Vicky.

Sissy turned the needle on the soldier and stabbed him in the stomach. The guard was so strong and powerful that, even after being stabbed, he grabbed Sissy and sank his teeth into her throat. Sissy gasped for air. As his stomach bled, the guard began to lose his strength and Sissy fell free from his grasp.

She tried to stand but couldn't. When she saw that the guard was dead she was relieved. She pulled herself over the hill. The blood from her neck soaked the ground. Sissy whispered, "Ronnie. Ronnie. I am back."

She crawled a few more steps and collapsed. The wind brushed her fur, but her body moved no more.

Eight needles rushed in towards Cookie.

Spence yelled, "If it jumps, point your needles to the ceiling. It's got to come back down. If it jumps over to one side, surround it again. If it tries to grab your needle, hold on to it as long as you can and the rest of us will stab it. Whoever stabs the squirrel first will be the hero."

Spence and his soldiers moved in closer. "All together, one step forward. Now one step to the left, now one more step to the left."

Cookie focused her attention on Spence. She tried to kick Spence, but he was waiting for an attack and dodged out of the way. As she swept her tail around to knock the soldiers down, Spence quickly shouted, "Jump two steps back."

He knew if one of them fell down Cookie would have an opening to get out or attack. Spence's soldiers were good. When Cookie moved slightly forward, the soldiers moved with her. She tried to sweep them again with her tail, but they automatically jumped back.

Cookie knew she would have to use unusual tactics. She had seen the Black Belt demo team practice a technique where the student being attacked would run toward the wall and push off the wall to jump back and counterattack the chaser.

Cookie had not used the needle Sissy gave her as a weapon yet. She didn't want to use it, since a needle killed Andy.

Cookie tried to jump out of the circle, but as soon as she moved, they surrounded her again as she expected.

She took a deep breath and jumped near the wall. They moved to surround her again, but she kicked off the wall and jumped to the side. As she landed, in the corner of her eye Cookie saw Ronnie and one of his men watching through the rags in the opening.

Cookie refocused. She kicked one soldier in the back, knocking him into another soldier. The circle was broken. Two soldiers were down now, and the circle no longer had strength.

Cookie tried to emphasize her attack at Spence. He was the leader. If she could knock him down, no one would be in control of the other soldiers.

She leapt towards Spence, but he dodged to the side, extending his needle as he lunged. "I stabbed it!" Spence had stabbed Cookie in her limp arm. "Rush in NOW! Kill the squirrel!"

Once she realized there was no pain in her arm, she punched Spence in the face with the other hand and then grabbed him by the neck. As she spun Spence around in the direction of his rushing soldiers, two needles simultaneously stabbed Spence's body.

Spence fell to his knees. The soldiers that had stabbed him stood stunned in disbelief. The other soldiers dropped their needles. Spence grabbed the arm of a soldier standing nearby and whispered, "Captain, tell my wife to avenge my death. Ronnie must die."

Spence's body fell limp at the Captain's feet.

Ronnie and his friends climbed through the opening and watched. Cookie didn't know how long Ronnie was there, but she could tell by his face that he had heard

Spence's wish.

Cookie allowed the unarmed soldiers to carry Spence and the old man's bodies out along with the other injured soldiers. However, she did not allow them to take their needles with them.

After all the soldiers were gone, Ronnie finally spoke, "Let me see your arm." Ronnie pulled the needle from Cookie's arm. "Are you in pain?"

"No. Luckily this is my injured arm." Cookie rubbed her bleeding arm as she explained.

Ronnie looked Cookie in the eyes. "I'm sorry for my rudeness. I blamed you for Andy's death and everything. Please forgive me."

"Let's forget about the past. The future is more important, isn't it? Has Sissy come back yet?"

"No. We'll have to rescue her. Let's go."

Ronnie, his soldiers, and Cookie climbed out of the vent.

Cookie had been trapped in the attic for so long. But now she could climb out with the yarn. Once she got out of the vent and onto the rooftop, fresh air filled her lungs, the stars filled her eyes, and the sounds of the night filled her ears like music. The world seemed as amazing and wonderful as the first day she went outside with her family.

Ronnie led the way through the darkness towards Spence's shopping center.

When they arrived at Spence's shopping center, the Captain came out unarmed. "What do you want, Ronnie?"

"I want Sissy back."

"What are you talking about? Sissy has already escaped."

"You are lying. Let me talk to Vicky."

"Wait here."

The Captain knocked on the wall outside of Vicky's room. "Mrs. Spence, Ronnie has come to see you. He is asking for his sister back, but I told them she already escaped."

Vicky did not come to the opening. Her voice trembled with tears and misery, "I don't want to see his face at all. My father and my husband are dead because of Ronnie. I don't want to be near him. Let the guard who watched Sissy tell them."

The Captain brought the guard to the main entranceway.

Ronnie spoke with the guard, but he told the exact same story.

The guard insisted. "She left. She ran away while Mrs. Spence was sick. By the way, Mrs. Spence visited her two times. She cared about her a lot. She told me that when Spence came back she was going to make her free. Now you should leave and respect her grief."

Vicky was very upset and angry. She saved Sissy's life for Ronnie, but Ronnie killed her husband and father. She couldn't believe it. She blamed Ronnie for everything. Her feelings of sympathy for Ronnie had become feelings of hatred. She couldn't believe the mind could change that quickly.

When she married Spence she knew Spence was a little bit tough and aggressive, but he didn't deserve to die. And the more she thought about her father, the angrier she became. As Spence's father-in-law, how could he avoid Spence's fight with Ronnie? Now it was too late.

Vicky couldn't stop her tears. She wished Ronnie were dead too. When the Captain returned to inform her that Ronnie had left, she called to the captain and hysterically ordered, "You must avenge Spence's death. You must kill Ronnie. Do not show your face again until he is dead!" Vicky gripped her stomach. This time the pain was real. The baby was coming.

On the way back to their shopping center, one of Ronnie's men found Sissy's body on the hill under a bush. Ronnie shook Sissy, but her body was cold. Ronnie cried, "Who did this to you, poor little sister?"

Cookie couldn't say a word. She was choking on tears. Even some of Ronnie's men were sobbing, because they knew their cowardice had caused Sissy's death.

Not far from that place, they spotted the guard's dead body that still had a needle in his stomach. Ronnie figured that they killed each other during Sissy's escape. Ronnie couldn't believe this tragedy. If Sissy had not tried to escape, she may still be alive.

As they placed Sissy's body near the area where she said goodbye to Andy, Ronnie cried, "Why do these things have to happen?"

Chapter Nine

The next day, Cookie's attic room became a small martial arts school. Mice of different shapes, sizes, and ages turned out for the first class. All of Ronnie's family, friends, and neighbors came to learn. Even the mice children, too small to train, came to sit and watch. Cookie lined everyone up in five rows of six. Then Cookie cleared her throat.

> Please, everybody sit down in your spots. I know some of you are here to learn how to fight, but that is not the true spirit of the martial arts. The truth is we are learning about ourselves. We are all different, but we all have the same goal—to find out who we are. I'm still learning who I am—and besides, I am not yet a Master.
>
> I have learned an important truth through my injury. The enemy hawk caught me because he probably needed me to feed his baby birds. And

because I escaped, his babies might not have had dinner. You see, as long as we live, there will always be killing and surviving. We are a part of the food chain. We eat and we are eaten. It's a continuous circle. But we are trying to survive as long as we can. That's what we have to accept as our destiny.

In truth, I don't have the right to teach you, but Ronnie was so persistent, I couldn't refuse. I will never forget what Ronnie's family has done for me. Without their help, I wouldn't be here. I really appreciate them. And for all of you, I will do my best.

I know that some of you want to learn how to kick and punch. Some want to learn how to use weapons. Some probably want to learn to defend themselves against weapons. Some want to find inner peace. I will do my best to help you reach your goal in martial arts and in life.

The Master emphasizes five categories called the Grandmaster's Signature System.

The first category focuses on theory, technique, principle, and performance. Inside this category are the basics, forms, and sparring.

The second category is conditioning, health, and fitness. This emphasizes basic health.

The third category develops energy while providing fun, excitement, and relaxation. This motivates us to continue our practice.

The fourth category deals with special functions, demonstration, and team building. This category helps us build strong social connections so that we are not isolated from others.

The final category develops character, values, morals, confidence, and positive attitude. This final category brings us to inner peace.

As Cookie talked, everyone listened quietly. Ronnie's eyes were wide open. He was surprised about Cookie's knowledge and experience. He realized that his world was so small, and that there was so much more beyond the world he knew. Ronnie was ashamed of his behavior and hatred towards Cookie. He was beginning to respect Cookie. When he came here, he only wanted to learn how to fight, but now he wanted to learn beyond fighting.

Everyone stand up. First, we have to open our joints by stretching. It is good for our health and for making power and strength. Circular movements are better for opening joints. Let's move our ankles in a circular clockwise motion, turn a few times. Now let's move them counterclockwise. Next let's move our knees, hips, shoulders, wrists, and neck.

Now let's sit down and stretch our legs and arms. Try to touch your nose to your knees. Now stretch up to the ceiling, arch your back. Move your legs apart in a straddle position. Touch your nose to the floor between your legs. This will help you kick higher and faster. Okay, stand up.

Stand with your feet two times shoulder width apart. Your toes should be pointing forward and your knees bent with your back straight. This is called Horseback Riding Stance. The purpose of this stance is to develop your big muscles.

Whenever you punch or kick, you must use big muscles first. This creates a lot more power. When you make a good Horseback Riding Stance, drop your hips as much as you can. Grab the floor with your toes. Try to relax your upper body. Try to punch.

Cookie moved in and out of the lines, helping and advising the mice on how to improve their technique. The mice were eager to learn and followed Cookie's every instruction.

Let's develop our reaction power. That is very important. While one hand punches, pull the other back as if you where executing an elbow attack behind you. When you relax your shoulders and waist, this helps to create power.

Do not punch with the arm alone. Beginners tend to tense their shoulders. You must relax your shoulders to connect your energy and power. Repetition will teach you correct movement.

When you make contact with an object, you should be tense momentarily and exhale deeply from your abdomen. Always put your tongue on the roof of your mouth. That will help your breathing and energy circulation. Everything else depends on how much you practice.

Let's finish class. The martial artist always shows respect by bowing. So let's stand up straight and

> bend our neck down. Very good, some of you will be sore tomorrow, but don't give up. Thank you.

The room exploded with applause. Everyone clapped.

Cookie blushed. Her first class was a success. She felt like a good teacher.

She remembered the Master had said,

> I teach you as if today was the last class of my life. That's how I can do my best. So you should think of today as the last workout in your life. Only then can you be your best.

Cookie decided she would always do her best for them.

For the next several weeks, Cookie taught them everything she learned. Of course, they could not copy everything. Their tails were not as strong and powerful as Cookie's tail. But they could use their whole bodies as well as both arms. Overall, Cookie thought they were all good standing martial artists.

Cookie remembered the Master telling his students,

> One day you will become a Master and carry martial arts on to the next generation. I am still following in my Grandmaster's footsteps as a student just like you follow in my footsteps for guidance. This will continuously happen.
>
> One day, when you become a Master, your students will follow in your footsteps like a circle with no beginning and no end. That's why in martial

arts, traditionally the beginners start with the 9th grade as White Belt.

When they are promoted, they become 8th grade then 7th grade until they become 1st grade. Then they become a Black Belt and then the rank system changes from small to bigger: 1st degree becomes 2nd degree until 9th degree.

One time I asked my Grandmaster to explain why the color belt system goes from bigger to smaller. He said, "9th to 1st and 1st to 9th represents a cycle of life. Martial arts represent life. Just like a son becomes a father and the father becomes a grandfather. The person does not change, but the title changes."

He told me that in the color belt stages, we work on getting over bad habits one by one. That's why the numbers get smaller. However, in the black belt stage, numbers get bigger as we add good habits one by one. In martial arts, the ranking system is a wonderful thing for setting and reaching goals.

Ronnie trained and practiced harder than any of the others. But in his mind, he couldn't erase what Cookie had said in the first class about inner peace. The more his martial arts improved the more he was frustrated about not yet finding inner peace. He wanted to ask Cookie about this, but he was afraid Cookie would think he was weak.

Ronnie could even see that his mother's attitude was more positive and calmer due to her training. She seemed stronger than ever before. Ronnie couldn't understand what was wrong with him.

As Vicky held her baby, she suddenly felt like the loneliest mother in the world. Spence Jr. looked so much like his father. Vicky now had to be a mother and a father to him, raise him, and protect him. His success would be her success. He was her only hope for the future.

Vicky became more hysterical and frantic after Spence Jr. was born. Everyone worried about her and her baby. She now blamed the Captain for her father's death. She thought the Captain should have stopped her father from going with them to Ronnie's shopping center. Vicky even held the Captain responsible for Spence's death. How could the Captain be alive and the leader be dead?

The Captain knew what she wanted. She wanted Ronnie dead. But the Captain knew he was not good enough to go back and fight that monster squirrel. The Captain tried to avoid Mrs. Spence until he could come up with a plan. Just thinking about that monster kicking, jumping, and spinning made the Captain weak in the knees.

The Captain decided it was best to catch Ronnie alone and fight one on one. For the next few days the Captain watched and waited outside of Ronnie's shopping center. The Captain noticed that Ronnie came out each night alone to the bushes to pick up a rock. He knew this would be his only chance.

That night the Captain waited again in the dark bushes. And just as he hoped, he saw Ronnie darting across the parking lot towards the bushes.

Ronnie was energized as he rushed across the parking lot to collect another rock like the old-day martial artists. He already had a small pile. Whenever he added to his pile he felt great. Some days he picked up several rocks, which meant he worked out and practiced several times that day. Today Ronnie was picking up two rocks.

The Captain tightened his grip on the needle. Ronnie walked right to the bush in front of the captain. The Captain jumped out of the bush and stabbed at Ronnie's stomach. Simultaneously, without thinking, Ronnie dodged the needle and spun around, grabbing the Captain's needle and sweeping his leg.

The Captain crashed to the ground. Ronnie was more surprised than the Captain, because he didn't realize he could throw an opponent so easily. When he realized his rocks were still in his hand, he smiled with confidence.

If this situation had happened before Ronnie began studying martial arts, he knew his only thought would have been to kill the soldier. However, Ronnie didn't want to kill him. He felt sorry for him. Ronnie was beginning to think that this true confidence was changing his character and values.

The Captain looked puzzled.

Ronnie threw the needle deep into the bushes. "Why do you want to kill me? I don't understand. The war is over. Do you want to continue like this? I thought you were the Captain. Why?"

"Don't ask questions. I'm the loser; you can kill me."

"No, I don't want to kill you. Killing is not the

answer." Ronnie grabbed the Captain's arm to help him up. "Captain, I don't want to harm you. I don't hate you. The last fight was nothing personal. Why do you want to start a fight again? Must one family be completely destroyed?"

"Vicky ordered me here to kill you."

"Captain, I don't believe you. Vicky wants me dead?"

The captain nodded his head. Ronnie was stunned.

"If you don't kill me, Vicky will send me again or other soldiers until you are dead. She is hysterical."

Ronnie had always taken comfort in the thought that even though Vicky had married and moved away at least she was still near his territory. He and Vicky could see the same stars, breathe the same air, and taste the same snow. Now she wanted him dead. A black curtain began to close in his mind, and behind it loving memories of Vicky. Ronnie began to see that he had no future here.

"Captain, you can go. Tell Vicky that I will leave this place until she feels comfortable. I was already planning to leave, since there is no hope of peace here. I wish her the best. Tell her I still love her and that my love for her has never been replaced. That may never happen. Tell her that even when we found Sissy dead, I never blamed her."

"What do you mean Sissy is dead? She escaped."

"Captain, she was killed by one of your guards just over the hill not far from here. You go back to Vicky and tell her my honest feelings about her and the situation. There is no reason that she and I have to fight anymore." Ronnie patted the Captain on the shoulder.

The Captain saw that Ronnie's eyes were filled with tears. "Okay, I will try." The Captain ran all the way back to Vicky, never stopping to look back.

Vicky screamed, "Captain, is Ronnie dead?"

"No, Mrs. Spence, I couldn't kill him. I tried to stab him but he was so fast. He took my needle and threw me to the ground."

"You could not handle one mouse. How can you come back alive and unhurt?"

"I found out that Sissy was killed by one of our guards when she was trying to escape. She killed the guard too. They killed each other."

Vicky gasped, "Are you sure that Sissy is dead?"

"Yes. I didn't see Sissy's body, but I know Ronnie wouldn't lie to me. By the way, Ronnie wanted me to give you a message. He is going to move away to make peace between our families. Oh, and he still loves you."

Vicky's knees gave way. "What? That's what he said?"

"Yes, ma'am." The Captain carefully helped Mrs. Spence up again.

"Captain, I understand you did your best. Thank you. Rest well."

When Vicky went back to her room, the news about Sissy and the message from Ronnie overlapped in her mind. She wished Ronnie was there to hold her. They could cry for Sissy until their tears were all gone. She knew once Ronnie left home he would never come back and she would never see him again.

When she married Spence, she missed Ronnie a lot, but she always took comfort in the fact that Ronnie was nearby. She tried to hide her feelings from Spence, but he always knew.

Vicky sobbed into her hands. Her face was soaked with tears.

She lifted Spence Jr. gently into her arms and cried harder. Vicky rocked Spence Jr. in her arms as she walked outside to look at the stars. The stars were shining the same as yesterday and she knew they would shine again tomorrow.

Knowing Vicky wanted him dead, Ronnie's feet dragged back to the shopping center. All his energy was gone. He had completely lost his appetite. Ronnie knew Cookie was ready to find her family, and the situation with Vicky made this the perfect time for them to leave. Ronnie knew that when Spence Jr. grew up there could be more trouble if he stayed. The best thing for his mom, his friends, and his neighbors would be if he left.

Ronnie sat down next to his mom. "Mom, I must leave with your permission. I have to help Cookie find her family. Without her help, our family and friends would not be here now. Spence is dead, so he cannot harm this shopping center or us anymore."

"Ronnie, I understand what you are saying. Helping friends is important, but you are my only son. If you go, why should I live? Please don't go."

"Mother, it won't take too long. It could be a couple

days or a couple of weeks. She needs her family too. They are waiting for her return. It's been a long time since the hawk took her. I promise I will be back as soon as possible."

"Andy went out and never came back. Sissy went out and never came back. Now you want to go out. You don't even know where you are going! What about me? If you love me, stay beside me. I won't live long, I am old."

"Mom, let's both think about it one more day. Okay?"

Ronnie couldn't sleep that night. He knew Cookie was a good fighter, but she didn't have outdoor experience. She might not survive by herself. Predators were not the only danger. From Ronnie's point of view, knowing how to find food was more important. Cookie had no experience with this. Ronnie felt he should go with her to help her. Even if it took her the rest of her life, Ronnie knew Cookie would search to find her family.

As Ronnie crawled through the opening into Cookie's room, he found her alone, preparing for class.

Ronnie cleared his throat. "Could I ask you a question?"

"Sure."

"Cookie, can you tell me how to find inner peace?"

"Ronnie, I think about that every day, too. The Master taught his students that without true love in their hearts they could not find inner peace. He taught that Love is B.E.S.T. B stands for **b**lessing. E stands for encouraging. S stands for supporting. T stands for touching. I guess inner peace depends on whether our heart is opened or closed. A lot of times we are not able to love others because we cannot yet love ourselves. If you know how to love yourself, then you can love others. Then we will be able to give others our love and fertilize our development of inner peace. In other words, passion is another form of inner peace. People think inner peace is soft like sea foam, but it can be solid like the strength of a rock. That's why some people believe that confidence fertilizes inner peace."

Ronnie thought quietly on what Cookie said. He was in awe of the Master's knowledge and Cookie's loyalty to the Master.

Ronnie told Cookie about his encounter with the Captain and Vicky's orders. "Cookie, I have to leave this place; otherwise the war will never end. When I leave, I want to take you with me to help you find your family. My mom doesn't want me to leave, but she doesn't know the whole situation. I don't want to explain Vicky's feelings to her."

"Ronnie, I think you should explain everything to your mom. It will make her feel better. You don't want to explain the situation with Vicky to your mom because of your pride."

"I guess you are right. I was thinking about myself, my image. I will explain everything to her. Thank you, Cookie. I'll go talk with her right now."

Ronnie explained everything to his mom.

His mom was shocked to hear about Vicky's orders

to have him killed. "My son, I understand why you have to leave. I hope you will come back home soon. Never forget, I'm always waiting for you. Poor son, when are you going to leave?"

"With your permission, I would like to leave as soon as possible, maybe tomorrow morning."

"My son, why not stay one more day and then leave the day after tomorrow?"

"Mom, I will be okay." Ronnie put his arm around his mom. "You know I can take care of myself. My friends will treat you well and look out for you. I promise you that one of these days I will be back. If I find a better place, I will come back for you."

"Son, I like this place. My parents were born here, I was born here, you were born here, and there are so many memories here. This place is part of my life. I am too old to move."

"Will you think about it?"

As Ronnie's mom nodded tears filled her eyes. "I will pray for you."

Ronnie and Cookie decided to leave the next morning. Cookie decided to teach one last martial arts class in the morning.

The next morning, every mouse in the shopping center came to train, watch, or say goodbye. Everyone was full of energy and enthusiasm. Ronnie and his friends put their best into that lesson, as they did for every lesson. The floor was covered with sweat.

Cookie raised her hand and the room became still

and silent. She motioned the students to sit down in their places.

Cookie retold one of her favorite stories by the Master.

There was a monk, named Won Hyo, that lived in ancient times. He wanted to leave Korea and go to India to study about his religion. Well, in those days, there were no cars, airplanes, or trains. Won Hyo had to travel by foot through the mountains to get to India.

Midway in his journey, he became lost. He had no map, no compass, and he had no idea where he was. He ran out of food and water. Won Hyo became delirious and confused. He did not know how many hours or days had passed.

One night he passed over a hill and, to his disbelief, he came upon a small pond. He couldn't believe it. There was even a small bowl next to the pond to drink from. He dipped the bowl into the water and drank. The cool water was delicious. He had never tasted water so good. Bowl after bowl, he filled his stomach with water. After filling his stomach, he fell asleep exhausted.

As Won Hyo awoke the next morning, he felt that he had regained his strength. He grabbed the bowl and sat up to drink from the pond. Won Hyo couldn't believe his eyes.

He saw that the pond was contaminated with the bodies of dead, mutilated animals. The water was covered in scum and smelled like sewage. The bowl in his hand was an animal's decomposing skull.

Won Hyo began to throw up over and over until his stomach was empty.

The average person would probably complain about the bad luck of drinking the dirty water. But not Won Hyo. He looked for understanding in life and religion. He was different. He was looking for the Do—the right way. What was the right way to look at this matter?

When he was thirsty and desperate, the water was delicious. When his stomach was full and his strength restored, that same water was disgusting. Why did he feel different about the same pond?

It is easier to look at our own situation and complain or blame someone or something else. If you look at life with a negative attitude, then it will be continuously miserable. But if you look at life with a positive attitude, then there is room for growth and change.

Do you realize that that dirty pond water saved Won Hyo's life? It restored his energy and strength. Without it he would have surely died. Won Hyo returned to Korea and became the greatest monk of his time, and his legacy still lives on today. Won Hyo taught us that our attitude is more important than our perception.

This attitude is the true spirit of a Black Belt. A true Black Belt no only wears a black belt around the waist but tries hard to overcome daily obstacles with a positive attitude.

The students and spectators burst into applause. Cookie bowed and shook hands with everyone. After class, the students gathered around Cookie. They gave her a farewell present wrapped in old newspaper.

Cookie looked at Ronnie, who shrugged. Ronnie knew nothing about the surprise gift. The students hugged Cookie and told her not to open it until she left.

Ronnie and Cookie said their final goodbyes to everyone.

Everyone knew that Ronnie's mom was trying to hide her tears.

After everybody said goodbye, Cookie stood alone. The big, empty room seemed bigger than ever before.

Cookie was sad to leave. As she thought about Andy and Sissy, tears swelled in her eyes. Cookie couldn't believe all that she had been through, all that she had learned, and all that she had overcome. She knew she was stronger and wiser because of all that had happened to her.

Cookie made up her mind to try to find her family, but she wasn't sure this was really possible. This was frustrating to think about. Then she thought of how the Master had spoken of the five elements of fullness: self, image, number, thought, and relationship. The awareness of "fullness of self" entered her mind.

Cookie remembered that the Master said,

> A true Master must understand and practice these elements in daily life, otherwise they do not fully understand the Do (the right way). That's why this

is privately taught from Master to Master. Being full of self is seeing your self in others. So the more you help others the more you help yourself. This means realizing that you can have everything you want in life by helping enough other people get what they want.

Cookie began to feel she understood fullness of self. The other elements were still unclear. Now that she was leaving, she knew she would have to teach herself to understand those other elements.

Cookie knew that even if she never found her parents, the love she had for them could be shared with others, like Ronnie. She did not know the reason clearly, but she knew that she had to forgive the hawk in order to understand the five elements.

She took one last look downstairs. Everything was quiet. No one was there yet. She would always remember the teachings of the Master. Cookie smiled.... Finally...inner peace.

When Cookie and Ronnie reached the bushes, Ronnie turned to wave goodbye to his mom watching from the main entrance. Once they were deep into the forest, past Vicky's shopping center, Cookie opened her present.

She dropped the newspaper and froze. "How is this possible?" Cookie's voice shook with joy. She couldn't believe her eyes.

Ronnie smiled. "You deserve it. Let me tie it on you. Look, it's a perfect fit."

The attic above the martial arts school was still and quiet again as the light downstairs turned on. As the Master stepped into his office he noticed something different about his desk.

The small teddy bear that he kept on his shelf had fallen over. The Master picked up the bear and straightened its tiny martial arts uniform. Immediately the Master noticed something was missing from the bear's uniform.

"Where is my black belt?"

Printed in the United States
37309LVS00002B/340-441

9 781413 781328